Praise for *The Question*

"'The Question' answered beautifully! The animals come alive for the reader and offer a beautiful answer for us to consider—that humans and animals live on this planet together. We must embrace that wonderful relationship."
~ *Barb W. Chicago. IL*

"You have done a remarkable job in getting your message out there in a way that is thoughtful, intelligent and provoking. These are very difficult topics to broach, but you have managed to combine a rational presentation of facts with an entertaining story and touches of humor. No one who reads your words can be unaffected. There is so much to process! Your ideas will linger and, for those who are conscious and ready, offer a more expansive view of who we are and our place in the oneness of which we are all a part." ~ *Dorothy J. Taos, NM*

"It's a good time to ponder our relationship with our fellow animals. Probably our future on this planet relies on internalizing the fact that we are co-habitors all, connected and interdependent. This book brings that message home in a most imaginative and totally new way. It deserves a wide readership and deep discussion." ~ *Rose J. Chicago, IL*

"What a wonderful contribution you have made to the fascinating subject of the human-animal connection. Animals are intelligent, emotional beings, and we humans are just now starting to recognize this. Unfortunately, there are those who still don't recognize it. I hope your book will open not only their eyes but their hearts as well. Great job!" ~ *Sandy. Palm Beach, FL*

"An 'aha moment' crept up on me midway through the book, as animals are personified and great human thinkers are trivialized. Discover the contentment resulting from learning that the human animal is indeed ONE with the animal world." ~ *Jim K. Stuart, FL*

"Thank you for reminding me how my spiritual life is unmistakably enhanced by the animals around me AND reminding me of the animal in me." ~ *Emelia W. Boulder, CO*

The QUESTION

The QUESTION

What Happened to the Animal-Human Spiritual Connection?

By
JUDITH HENSEL

SIX DEGREES PUBLISHING GROUP

PORTLAND, OREGON

Six Degrees Publishing Group
5320 SW Macadam Avenue
Portland, Oregon 97239

First Paperback Edition 2012

ISBN: 978-0-9856048-0-6
Library of Congress Control Number: 2012939331

Inquiries may be made by emailing Permissions@SixDegreesPublishing.com

Publisher's note:
This is a work of fiction. Names, characters, places and incidents either are the product of the author's imagination or are used fictitiously, and any resemblance to actual persons, living or dead, business establishments, events or locales is entirely coincidental.

Cover illustration: *OM!* Montage-painting by Judith Hensel
© 2001 Judith Hensel
Cover Design: Judy Bullard Covers
Author Photo: Rhoda Pollack

Printed in the United States of America

1 3 5 7 9 10 8 6 4 2

I was there for a long time alone. And the sort of feeling that I got when I was out in the forest is that there's a little spark of this Great Spirit power in each living thing. And if it's a soul in us, then I think the chimpanzees also have souls.
— Jane Goodall

CONTENTS

ACT 1

Getting Started

PROLOGUE
Setting the Stage

Whether we are interested in the other animals or not, there is no doubt we share our lives with them. They are everywhere – flying overhead, meowing a greeting in the morning, buzzing at our window, swimming in our lakes and in the glass bowl on the kitchen counter. The other animals share the Earth we walk on, the air we breathe, and the food we consume. They are the food we consume. Whether we notice them or not, they are always here among us.

☙

THIS MORNING IN THE QUIET OF MEDITATION, my mind drifted to a memory that still haunts me. I wince as the scene opens. I am walking down a road in Jaipur being jostled by an endless stream of people. Wrapped in yards of cloth, they are faceless, flowing forms. The land is so dry that simply walking in the streets raises clouds of dust and sand. The sun floats like a red balloon caught in dusty, hot air.

Riders on Donkeys, bicycles, carts, motorcycles and contraptions with wheels maneuver their way through the crowd. Their horns, bells and whistles make a cacophonous din. We soon learned the din never stops day and night. I imagine the language they are shouting to get the crowd to move along is laced with obscenities as well as the name of Ram (God). There's no hurry. There's nowhere in particular to go.

Suddenly a Dog ran out into the busy street. I shouted, "Look out!" Too late. Hit by a bicycle, he crumpled to the ground. The horde stepped over him if he was blocking their way. As I pushed and shoved my way through the throng to help the poor creature, I wondered how the other animals living in the streets fared in such conditions. India's roads are filled with animals in awful shape endlessly searching for anything (any thing) to consume. Longhaired, skinny little Pigs and scraggly, sore-covered Dogs hide in alleyways to avoid the kids who throw rocks at them.

Considered sacred by the Hindus, long-horned Brahmin Bulls roam freely on the streets. An impossibly skeletal Cow found a corner where two clay walls meet and pressed his head into the crevice trying to find shade. My companions and I wondered where the giants went at night. We found out when we cut through a pitch-dark alley. Two were hovering together and bellowed their surprise when we accidentally bumped into them.

The Horses and Donkeys have no flesh or muscle tone. Just skin stretched over bones. The Horses are surprisingly small. Tiny in comparison to the Horses I've seen grazing in farm fields back home. The hapless creatures are switched non-stop with sticks forcing them to navigate the rocks imbedded in the roads. Their task is to pull loads ten times their size and many more times heavy. Once I saw a little Horse pulling a wagonload piled high with scrap metal. He pulled his load, all right. He stumbled and fell, but got up all right. Sticks hurt. Not right.

My traveling companions were surprised by my reaction over the plight of the animals. Their interest was in the street people, especially the children. It's not that I didn't care about the people's hardships. I sincerely did. It's just that I've been sensitive to animal pain from a very young age. I think it has something to do with the other animals' vulnerability in the hands of humans. They have no real choice. We are in control.

Just recently, I recalled a childhood memory that reminded me how my feelings for the animals took root in my consciousness. I was a curious child. My curiosity got me into trouble when I was enticed by several older boys into the foundation of a house being built in our south side Chicago neighborhood. I thought they were my friends. The assault on my innocence altered my perspective about people well into my adulthood. At the age of six, curiosity was replaced by caution, and trust by fear and doubt.

I was fortunate to have a place to go to heal. Summers at my aunt and uncle's farm usually began like this. My aunt would pick me up at the train station and repeat over and over in the truck as we bumped along unpaved country roads, "Now, don't go taming those barn Cats! I don't want them in the house. Besides,

they have a job to do keeping the Mice from eating all the grain."
I wondered how little Mice could eat all that grain in uncle's silo,
but knew better than to debate with her.

I couldn't wait to see my friends! I'd race up the stairs,
throw my backpack on the bed and run to the barn to be with
my beloved Cats. We had a lot in common. Barn Cats didn't trust
people. I didn't either. I gained theirs by sitting quietly on that
dusty barn floor. Soon a young one would cautiously creep up to
me. I'd reach out to touch him but he'd run away. Another would
approach. She might let me touch her very gently. After several
days, the kittens climbed into my lap, and the older ones pressed
against me for pets. The rest of the summer would be filled with
our endless play.

Uncle's good old Cow provided nourishment for her Calf
and us. I loved going with him before dawn to her stall in that
chilly, muddy barn to collect our share of her morning milk. I
had to control my giggles when she peed on my dear uncle if
he didn't position himself a certain way under her udders. He'd
jump up and cuss many words (which I still use), hose himself off
and sit in the space she wanted him to be in the first place. Most of
all, I loved watching the Pigs happily rolling in the mud. I never
once connected any of my animal friends on that farm to the ham,
steak and eggs we ate.

There were many life lessons to learn from the animals on
that little farm. The free Chickens taught me about the pecking
order that I soon learned exists in the human world too. One
hapless Chicken was always at the bottom of their society. Her
head would be red and raw from the pecks of those who believed
they were higher up than she. I'd sit for hours throwing rocks to
deter the peckers. They'd always return to the poor lowly one.
My experience with those Chickens served me well as a teacher. I
was able to identify the kid "pecked on" in class and found ways
to guide the students' attention away from the misunderstood
one. Sometimes it worked.

When my parents picked me up at the end of the summer, I'd look
out the back window of our station wagon to see Aunt waving
her broom as she chased the Cats back to the barn. They easily
escaped her by a long run. "See you next year!" I'd shout. I swear

one of the Cats would stop and wave.

Nowadays, I can't leave my apartment without spotting dozens of animal species living in my neighborhood. Sparrows and Finches flit over the rooftops and gather in the bushes. Cat patiently waits in the grass for just one to land near him. No such luck today. Neighbor's Dog always runs to me with tail wagging expecting the biscuit she knows I have in my pocket just for her. Geese fly overhead rehearsing for their fall migration to warmer climes. Across the street, Hawk hunts from on high searching the open field. In a long forgotten hole under the creek bridge, Fox waits for dusk. Best time to hunt. Mouse stays undercover. (Safer to come out at night.) Rabbit cautiously reveals herself under my porch. Across the alley Butterflies and Bees compete for the pollen of a lone morning glory thriving on a battered fence. Hummingbirds sip sugar nectar from a jug suspended from someone's balcony. I call out my best imitation of "caws" to the Crows lined up on a lamppost. Sometimes they join the game and call back.

The animals have taken center stage in my thoughts no matter how hard I try to think about other matters. They are reminding me that their cousins are suffering and in pain at the hands of humans. I began to wonder if the reason for our treatment of the other animals can be found somewhere in our spiritual beliefs about them.

I contacted a favorite professor and invited myself to tea. Dr. Diana G. is a renowned professor of world religions and history. Her eyes reflect a woman of wisdom. Laughter is second nature to her. She is certain about her beliefs. I'm not certain of anything.

As I climbed up the stairs to her little apartment, I could hear her teapot whistling throughout the hallway. Another delicious hour with Earl Grey tea and ginger cookies was about to begin. After the usual hugs and small talk, we sat down.

Our conversations make me think of two actors in a play. I am standing alone center stage delivering a soliloquy. At least I think I'm alone. But she's there. Always there with me. I picture one of us facing stage right, and the other facing stage left. We are tied together at our waists by a golden chord. Joined tightly, we can't stray very far from each other. She speaks her thoughts at the same time I speak mine. I'm sure an audience would be confused by our jabberwocky.

Our discourse usually takes us deep into ideas we probably should never tackle because we disagree on just about everything. Yet we honor each other's opinions and our debates strengthen our friendship. Little did I know that on this particular visit our conversation would become the embarkation point of an adventure that would change both our lives forever.

I was nervous about today, and asked her if I could tape our discussion. "Record our conversation?" she asked. "This must be important." Noticing my mood, she said, "OK 'Q', what's on your mind?"

I answered, "I've begun writing a book addressing a question that keeps me awake at night."

She asked, "What is this burning question?"

I said, "I can't understand why a vast majority of animal species are disconfirmed in our lives to the point of neglect and abuse. I believe that a spiritual connection between humans and animals did exist at one time. I have a feeling it was broken somewhere in history. My research indicates that religions have a lot to do with the disconnection."

She looked down at her cup. She always does that when she disagrees with me or wants to change the subject. Talking to the top of her head, I said, "The doctrines of the religions focus on the relationship between *humans* and God. The animals are missing. I'm trying to find out what happened. It seems one's religious beliefs influence . . ."

The former nun slammed her teacup down onto its saucer. A spoon hopped off the table and skittered behind my shoe still shaking. Poor spoon. My mind raced to outguess what she's going to say. Get there first with a good answer. "Oh no you don't!" she said, trying to stay calm. "It seems most of our conversations become debates about my religion. Can't we talk about something else? I certainly nicknamed you right when you were my student! You never have stopped asking "Q"uestions, have you Q? Now you want me to do what? Include animals in my prayers? I don't have time to fit them in! There's so much to speak to God about. If saving the animals is what you want to do, then I'm OK with it. But count me out if you're asking me to get involved!"

The tone of her voice rattled me enough to knock over the

creamer onto the plate of cookies. After cleaning up the mess (thank goodness there were more cookies) I said, "I'm not challenging you or your religion, Diana, and the animals don't know what a prayer is. But when I see a Dog harshly whipped and a Cat left outside all night in the freezing cold, I want to help them as much as you do people. Just yesterday, friends invited me to visit their new home in Door County, Wisconsin. I couldn't accept because I couldn't bear to see the Calf houses installed on those postcard-perfect dairy farms. The newborn Calves are cramped into pens and left alone in the dark for weeks."

Diana looked out of her window. "Why do the farmers do that?"

I replied, "To make their flesh more tender. The farmers take the babies from their mothers as soon as they are born to begin the process of 'veal preparation.' The usual procedure is to place them in small pens and chain them by the neck so they can't move and build muscle. After three to six months, they are taken out of their confines. Unable to walk, the unfortunate animals fall to the ground quite helpless. I can't pass a food animal farm without wondering if Calf (*veal*) houses are somewhere on the property."

She interrupted, "Stop it! Those farmers have to make a living! They have their own problems. Why don't you drop the animal cause and take care of your fellow human beings if you're looking for something to do?"

"I can't, Diana," I said. "It's as if the animals are talking to me somehow. Religious laws were made to serve human needs. How could any sort of laws be written in the name of God to protect the animals used for food and their skin to be made into covers for our furniture and shoes?"

Jumping up, Diana began to clear the table, "Here you go! We are not five minutes into the conversation, and you're challenging religions again. Aren't you interested in anything else? What makes you the revisionist of our history? I'm not in the mood to defend God today!"

She put another pot of water on to boil. "Give me a chance to think," she mumbled. I checked to make sure the tape recorder was still recording. Without turning around from the stove she said, "You make it sound as if the writers from ancient times were bad guys. That they split human consciousness away from the animals on purpose. I think they weren't sophisticated enough to sit at their scribing desks and say, 'Let's take the animals out of God's plan.' Women were written out of God's plan too, especially in the Middle East. The authors never dreamed there would be consequences thousands of years later. All they knew was they were in power and were going to stay there. We can't cry over spilled milk."

"Spilled milk? What does that mean?" I asked, adding a spoonful of honey in what was left of my tea. "Lately, I've been interested in the idea of reincarnation. Millions of people believe that when their body dies, their soul or spirit returns to live in every conceivable life form. It might take millennia for the soul to realize the purpose of its existence. Once it does, many believe their soul will be freed from the cosmic circle of life and rest in peace with the Source of all that is. It seems to me that reincarnation is a form of Universal justice."

Diana's eyes glazed over. Is she listening? I kept talking anyway. "The authors of the early Vedic literature unknowingly used a basic law of physics when they described karma: *For every action there is an opposite and equal reaction.* For instance, if we want to avoid pain in our next lifetime, we should stop giving pain to all creatures in this life. I prefer this arrangement rather than the alternative: living one lifetime with two after-death options taught to me by my Sunday school teacher. At the rate I was going, I was going to Hell by the time I was ten years old because of all my mischief. That just doesn't appeal to me."

She laughed. "Well then, can my soul come back to live in the body of a Calf? I'm not kidding! If I eat veal, will I come back as a Calf? It seems to me you need to clarify your question. I assume you are zeroing in on the animal world to find some flaw in religions." The teakettle finally sounded its piercing whistle. She poured boiling water over fresh tealeaves and carried the pot back to the table. We silently refilled our cups and carefully sipped the steaming brew.

"That's not it," I said. "Religion would be too easy of an answer. I'm talking about one's 'Spirituality' which encompasses all of an individual's beliefs. The way I see it 'Religion' and 'Spirituality' are not interchangeable concepts. Spirituality is a person's self-secret beliefs and attitudes as shown by his and her's behavior toward others. This would include their actions toward the other animals. Using this definition, whether we are aware of it or not, every thought we think and every action we take is spiritual action."

Frowning, Diana leaned forward. Before she could interrupt I said it another way, "As spiritual beings, we act out our beliefs. Our behavior toward others is what we *truly* believe about them deep inside ourselves."

She said, "You're not serious are you, Q? Even though I understand the concept, I can't agree with your premise. Spirituality has always been associated with religion. It is about our most elevated thoughts connecting us to God."

I responded, "I think our religious beliefs are just one segment of a broader system of beliefs we acquire through our experiences with the 'heroes' or 'winners' in our lives." Diana shifted in her seat, never taking her eyes off me.

"Let me explain?" I said quickly. "Our heroes can be the people who parented us, our peers, family, friends, teachers, and even the guy bagging our groceries. Our heroes' actions may not 'elevate' our moral consciousness and often conflict with the actions of the other 'heroes.' Nonetheless, whoever 'wins' a situation impacts our behavior. For instance, the way people treat the other animals is a good example of conflict between beliefs and actions." Diana's head is down again. Uh Oh!

I hurriedly continued, "Let's say a cowboy at a rodeo harshly whips a Horse and wins a lot of prize money for staying on the animal for the longest seconds. The cowboy's win might be transferred into a boy's belief system when the boy notices he can 'win' by smacking his Dog, and she obeys. A science teacher might influence the boy's spiritual sensibilities when she refuses to teach animal experimentation in her classroom. Her defiant stance before the school board gets her in trouble for not following the state's educational requirements. The boy's teacher 'won' his admiration for standing up for her beliefs, but the state 'won' the game.

"On Sundays, his parents take him to 'canned hunts' to shoot Doves released from cages. The experience integrates into the boy's innermost belief system when he learns how easy it is to kill trapped animals. Well, you get the picture. All these experiences with the 'winners,' or 'heroes' he encounters in his life influence the boy's spiritual connection with animals."

Diana looked up, propped her chin in her hand and stared at me incredulously. Undeterred, I added, "As the boy matures, his experiences with the other animals blur together. The system is eccentric because some of the heroes' actions in a particular situation conflict with another heroes' actions in the same situation. The boy's spiritual self is triggered when a circumstance calls for a specific kind of behavior or action toward an animal as based on the whole picture."

Applauding, Diana said, "Nice story, Q! You sure know how to distort tradition! You have a gift for twisting semantics!" She pushed her chair away from the table indicating she wanted the discussion to be over.

I quickly responded, "Tradition can be moot if it becomes an excuse for retaining ideas that are no longer applicable in people's lives, don't you think?" She glared at me but stayed in her seat.

I said, "I'm almost through trying to explain my book thesis to you, Diana. Please be patient with me? I'm not trying to rattle you or challenge your personal beliefs. I'm in a dilemma. I need your wisdom right now. Will you help me?" Her eyes softened. Folding her hands in her lap, she nodded.

Assured, I continued, "Not all people mistreat animals. In fact most of the people who have animals living with them adopt them as beloved members of their family. All over the world, millions of men and women believe that behaving toward animals with respect and compassion is a vital law of Nature. Some are dedicating their lives to protecting animals from people who don't believe as they do. In my way of thinking, the animal guardians' behavior is as 'spiritual' as those dedicated to helping people."

Shaking her head, she said, "You're talking about a complete shift in society's perception of what 'spirituality' is, especially when it comes to people's beliefs about animals. This is where we're going with this discussion, right? Your idea is impossible!"

I responded, "My friend, societal change is possible. Gloria Steinem and countless women in spite of threats and harsh criticism changed the established view that men by virtue of their gender have the natural right to control their families, the laws, even religions. If aliens from outer space read a history book written before the 1970's, the text would refer to both men and women as 'men.' They would think that the Earth was populated by one gender. Male.

"Isn't it time to bring the animals in from the cold? For starters, thousands of Horses, Mules and Oxen enabled people to settle the West. San Francisco's steep hills became dying hills when the hapless animals were forced to pull heavy loads up those muddy inclines. Ever read about these brave beings in your history books? I am certain the people controlling them noticed they felt pain, could think, had emotions . . ."

She interrupted, "Emotions? Can you prove that?"

"Of course I can!" I replied. "Don't go scientific on me. It's not your style. Can you prove there is a God?"

She looked at me over the top of her glasses and with a tinge in her voice said, "*Careful*, sister, you're already in dangerous territory with this conversation!"

Dangerous territory? Who should I be afraid of? Her? God? Maybe I *am* afraid! Cautiously, I continued, "There must be a correlation between how we care for each other and how we care for the other animals. It goes beyond concern for Sparrows hunted by Cats and people killing people. Maybe our discussion is meaningless. But if it is, then what's all this endless talk about our relationship with God the human psyche will not let go of?"

Ignoring my question, she asked, "Are you ascribing to animals a kind of ability to discern between right and wrong? Do animals have a moral center?"

I answered with another question. "Does morality indicate the presence of a soul? Is this where you are heading? If you want to talk about animal morality, we can only speak about what we observe. In *Ravens in Winter*, Bernd Heinrich describes how Ravens and Crows share the sparse food available to them during the harsh winter season. In fact, most wild animals share food and water when times are hard. I'd say their 'morality' is at a higher level than humans. Humanity's best wars have been waged during times of hunger for one side or the other."

"May I change the subject?" I asked. Diana looked relieved. Taking a deep breath, I plunged in. "Modern day theoretical physicists are speculating that the Universe might be expanding *consciously.* Most of their colleagues disagree with their mathematical theories, yet a growing number of people outside of the scientific community are finding the idea wonderful. However, new questions arise. If the Universe is conscious of itself, how does the possibility fit into the worldview of life or God? Who are we? Who are the animals? What is our relationship with all that exists?"

Diana sat quietly for a moment. "Does this group of scientists you are talking about include animal life in their theory? Are they saying that the other animals have the same God-like nature as humans? I don't see the connection between a lot of scientists' unproven theories and animals."

The golden cord tying us together at our waists began to loosen.

"Few societies make the connection between their 'God-like nature' and the nature of the animals," I said. "There's a tribe living somewhere in a rain forest that worships the Pig. The men stick a pointed spear through their god's throat and hold up his writhing body as they dance the night away celebrating his death. Can't they relate their god's cries with their own squeals when they are in pain? The Pig doesn't know what a god is. Let alone know why he must die such a horrid death. Perhaps this 'God-like nature' you speak of is somewhere in the character of a culture."

"Now I think you're humoring me," she said.

I described my sessions with an animal "Communicator." I asked her, "Does my Cat know about the God we humans are so interested in? The Communicator replied, 'Animals don't have to know about God. They are already 'there.' When I heard this, I knew I'd heard a universal truth. Animals don't sit around endlessly pontificating about God and whether what they are doing is 'sinful' or 'wrong.' They simply exist. They just are. They just be. Do you understand what I'm trying to say?"

Diana said, "I think so, although I find it absurd that anyone can 'communicate' with animals."

I described my interview with a respected zoo director in the Midwest who told me he too found the idea of 'animal communication' absurd. Then after thinking about it, he said, "I don't know about communicating with animals, but lately when I pass a cage, I sense the animals are speaking to me somehow. One might be saying to me, 'I want to play' and another might say, 'my water pan is empty.' I hear their 'voices' in my head long before I check to see if what I heard is actually what they are 'saying.' It usually is." He added, "I wonder if animals use telepathy to get our attention." Then he said, "I draw the line at Cockroaches. They'll never get my attention!"

Diana laughed. "I don't blame him!"

"Me too," I said. "Joanne Lauck Hobb's book *The Voice of the Infinite in the Small* gave me an appreciation of how dangerous it is for the smallest-animals-we-can-see to live out their life cycle as it is for the Elephant. The author advocates that Earth's miniature life forms are significant aspects of a vital principle of Universal Consciousness. For instance, Bee and Ant communities appear to behave as one collective body, not as individual animals.

"Charles Darwin discovered that Earthworms have cognitive abilities and experience their lives subjectively in his definitive study, *The Formation of Vegetable Mould through the Action of Worms with Observations on their Habits* (1881). His theory is rarely discussed in today's world of science. I wonder why." Diana put her head on the table. I couldn't decide whether she was stifling a giggle or making a point I didn't get.

Determined to finish, I said, "There's an interesting story about a holy man who allowed mosquitoes to feed on his blood so that they could survive. It is as marvelous and awful as any other story about people who sacrifice their lives for others."

Looking up with disgust, Diana said, "*Now* you've really lost me! Dying so mosquitoes can live? *Ugh!* Makes me itch just thinking about it!" We both shuddered.

"What about the less bothersome, yet martyred animals?" I asked. "How can people go to church in the morning, sing pious songs, and ask for forgiveness for their sins (toward humans or their God), and then go to a rodeo or circus in the afternoon and be entertained watching animals being beaten into submission or forced to perform tricks that are contrary to their physical capabilities?"

She interrupted, "What are you leading up to, Q?"

I paused a long minute before replying. "It seems to me that if the other animals were integral in our spiritual selves, we just might strengthen the laws that are supposed to protect them from abuse. Maybe countries worldwide would enforce humane treatment of all animals. Maybe would assure the food animals don't suffer as they do during the awful minutes their bodies are 'processed' into products while they are still alive." Hesitating, I laid my last card on the table. "Ideally, we might take a primal step toward finding the truth about who we truly are . . ."

That did it! Diana's voice began to rise. "Q! This isn't about animals! It's about philosophical and scientific concepts about the Universe. It's really kind of heavy. You're expecting me to enter deeply into something I cannot possibly relate to. That's kind of presumptuous! I don't know how to react to all this!"

Talking faster, I mentioned Joseph Campbell, renowned mythologist who spent his lifetime teaching fables about how the other animals affect people's spiritual lives.

"I'm sitting here with my mouth open!" she said. "I'm listening to you. But I'm not participating. I must not be a good listener. I guess I don't buy your premise. Your presumption that animals don't exist in our innermost consciousness is not true. Joseph Campbell was right. Animals have populated world mythologies from the beginning of human history. Every story the Native American Indians tell expresses their spiritual connection with animals in their everyday lives. The legend about the founders of Rome being raised by Wolves is told over and over again. Many myths are lessons about the interdependence of animals and humans."

Sipping her tea, she carefully chose her words, "For better or for worse, I prefer serving people. Probably because I do presume there is a hierarchy of intelligence in Nature." She paused, then said, "You're correct to say a person's beliefs and attitudes come from direct experience. Think about racism in this country. The barriers of the white fortresses had to be broken down before people realized that a fair and just life is essential for everyone. I cannot imagine the same thing will ever happen in our relationship with the animals."

"Why not?" I asked. "Is it because the animals can't speak for themselves? They don't stand a chance if the only way they can get through to us is to beat down our fortresses! They don't know how!"

Diana had grown weary of the debate. "You're trying from every angle to point me to your way of thinking about something which I don't have time (or want to take the time) to wrap my thoughts around."

I asked, "What would it take to bring the animals into your spirituality?"

She replied, "Take care of what is happening in Iraq and Afghanistan for me, will you? Heal all the old men and women in senior homes worrying about their social security and their medical problems, their aches and their pains, their loneliness. Take care of all that, and then I'll have more time for the animals. OK? Another cookie?"

FOR WEEKS, I asked friends, colleagues, neighbors and strangers (if the opportunity arose) to find out where they stood about animals in their spiritual lives. Many sided with Diana's viewpoint. Many agreed with mine. THE QUESTION remains on the table.

What happened to the animal-human spiritual connection?

ONE
Maybe

Mᴀʏʙᴇ ᴀ ɴᴇᴡ ᴡᴏʀʟᴅ ʜɪsᴛᴏʀʏ should be written crediting the role of the other animals for their contributions to human evolution. A history that describes deeper, more meaningful animal-human relationships other than hamburgers, Frisbees, and pulling heavy loads.

Maybe from the safety of the bush, first homo species learned to survive by observing the other animals. The animals knew which grasses and leaves would nourish them and where water could be found. (*Let's eat the same plants and follow the four-legged and winged ones to the water.*) The animals sensed when the seasons were changing and moved on when it was time to find food elsewhere. (*Better move on with them.*) They cry out in pain when they are hurt and heal their wounds by rubbing against certain plants. (*We cry out in pain when we are hurt. Let's rub against the same plants to feel better.*)

Early humans modified the actions of predators to suit their own special needs. They couldn't run as fast as the Cheetah, or grab its prey by the neck with their teeth to bring it down for a meal. But a rock made an excellent killing tool. (*The Leopards are right. A tree branch overhanging the Ibex trail makes a fine ambush site.*)

Perhaps 35,000 years ago, a woman excitedly returned to her tribe to report her encounters with an animal, but couldn't explain what she had seen. With that, she picked up a handful of red mud and smeared the outline of a full-size animal on the walls of the cave to get her story across. (The rest is art history.)

When did prehistoric peoples stop gnawing the bones of animals they scavenged to turn their faces toward the skies? When did they begin to wonder what caused the lightning to illuminate their cave walls? The waters to flow from here to there? Where did the animals foraging nearby (or chasing us) come from? Did we come from the same place?

Maybe the animals taught morality to humans. Could our proclivity toward what is "right" and "wrong" been inspired by watching the other animals' selfless behavior toward their own species? Bear defends her cubs to her death, or to the death of the animal that tries to take them. Wolves and many other species including birds, mate for life and exhibit gentle affection as well as fierce loyalty to their young. Unless life-threatening dangers are imminent that would seriously affect the safety of the entire herd, Elephants will not leave their wounded behind. Maybe the original human tribal laws were the same as the moral code of the other animals. *It is wrong to steal food or the mate of another. It is right to defend our families and territory to the death. It is good to bury our dead.*

Maybe someone in the tribe observed animals dreaming. Early homo species might have enjoyed a great laugh around the campfire watching their sleeping Dog kicking and growling as she chased Rabbit who had hopped into her dreams. Perhaps, someone in the tribe wondered, whether Dog has an unseen twin, a "spirit," dwelling inside her body that comes alive when she sleeps. Is it Dog's spirit that is growling and kicking while her body sleeps? What happens to that Rabbit when Dog wakes up? Maybe all Dog has to do to find that Rabbit again is to fall asleep. *Maybe we have a spirit that lives in our dreams too. Maybe our spirit sleeps when we wake up, and awakens when we fall sleep again.*

Did the death of tribal members or animals inspire another question about the "dream spirit?" What happens to the spirit dwelling in our dreams when the body stops moving and there is no breath? Does the dream continue? *Maybe the dead one's spirit lives in the dream world forever.*

Although prehistoric people left no written records, many archeologists have concluded they believed their spirits continued to live on after they died. Ancient gravesites contain bones of humans and animals buried together along with "supplies" of food and weapons. It would appear that first humans welcomed the animals to accompany them in the eternal dream.

The development of writing made it possible to record the ancients' oral histories that had been repeated over and over around the cave fires for millennia. Starting in the 4th millennium BCE, treatises about the relationship between humans and the other animals were set down. The following chronicles the belief that humans and the other animals exist together in an infinite state of Consciousness:

> "This One is . . . Brahman (the Infinite) –
> And This is . . . these five elements, viz. Earth, Air,
> Space, Water, and Fire.
> And This is . . . all these big creatures,
> together with the small ones, that are the procreators of others,
> viz. horses, cattle, men, elephants, and all the creatures that there
> are which move or fly and those which do not move.
> All these have Consciousness as the giver of their reality –
> All these are impelled by Consciousness.
> The Universe has Consciousness as its eye . . .
> Consciousness is Brahman – and Consciousness is its end."
>   Aitareya Upanishad III-i-3
>   (1200-900 B.C.) Vedic literature.

New generations of scribes revised the earlier myths to fit the needs of their times. They may have reasoned there is another worldview of "after life" other than animals and humans taking a long dream journey together. Was it the priests who closed off the dream bridge crossed by the other animals? Did the priests redefine the soul to be exclusively a human characteristic? Could the diminishment of the animals' place in religious texts be the very factor that continues to influence how people behave toward animals today?

Maybe the animals are missing in our spiritual lives because they aren't worth the consideration.

Two
No Turning Back

SLEEP HAS BECOME MY REFUGE. I'm reluctant to open my eyes and leave my night sleep-roam. Formless, my soul soars across marvelous other worlds. It is hard to leave the safety of sleep where I am surprised with images I could never imagine when I'm awake.

One morning, a delivery truck horn sounded in the alley below. Its blast broke up one of my loveliest dreams, and my soul reluctantly landed back into my body. I tried to recall the dream still lingering in my head, but forgot the details before it vaporized altogether.

Time to re-invent my existence. Forms assemble and settle into the space around me in the order I create them. My bedroom arranges itself so I won't be confused by the illusion. It always takes a moment or two to realize that I am alive! Alive! A life! Life! How can I express the feeling of being alive? The knowing trickles into my senses as I breathe breaths, scratch an itch, stretch a stretch, and smell a smell. Yes! I'm alive! On this fine morning, I am exhilarated by the thought.

As the truck rumbled away, the birds' chirping resumed. I don't hear their chatter until I remember to remember they are out there, although they've been talking to me long before dawn. They remind me that I'm never alone. I have so much company. For the first time in weeks I remember that our Earth teems with life forms as numerous as the stars in our galaxy.

I take a long breath. I hold up my hands and look at them and raise my arms to the ceiling to watch my fingers move. Bhapu, my constant companion, hops onto my stomach to remind me I am alive. He's been waiting for hours to tell me. "Yes, you are alive. So am I. What took you so long to figure it out?" Try as he may, he can't join me in my dreams. All he can do is get out of the way as I toss and turn this way and that. He does his best to stay close, first curling under one arm, then the next, and then back again. He must be exhausted trying to keep up with me. I stroke his soft softness. My loyal, furry friend.

He rolls on his back, pushing himself as close to me as he can. His purrs vibrate louder and louder. "Scratch me there and there!" Easy to please, easy to love, I promise him his every-morning promise. He will always be safe with me and never want for anything. It's the least I can do in return for his sharing his life with me.

I looked out of my window. There they are! Beyond the rooftops are Boulder's Flatiron Mountains worn down to angular rock formations during Earth's geological changes. During one of the changes, the Flatirons rested under ancient seas. I can almost see prehistoric water dwellers swimming across the sea-sky. Swimming across my room.

Now I see him! I imagine the dawn sun is lighting the horizon along the graceful Flatirons to reveal the shape of Southern Arapaho Indian chief Niwot's reclining body. The chief's tribe wintered in Boulder valley in the late nineteenth century until the Third Colorado Calvary took their land and their lives in what is called the Sand Creek Massacre. It is said that Chief Niwot stood in the middle of the battle with his arms folded, refusing to fight the white men he believed were his friends.

The animals enter my thoughts. I dive deeper into my mind as I scan the world for them. They're never far away these days. Some have names. Shadow, Lily, Beau, Bentley, Gracie, Tess. Then it happens. It always happens when I least expect it. I feel their presence and become them.

I become lowland Gorilla signing the language of the human deaf, "I love you," to my caretaker. Maybe if I show her I am able to communicate to her using human methods, she'll notice that I am an intelligent being. She knows I am from a dwindling tribe barely surviving in a rain forest. My family must move from their home as the fires are set closer and closer to their habitat. Maybe my caretaker will tell the world what she's learned from me. When she tells the world, will people believe her?

I am Gray Whale racing toward waters that have been my tribe's nursery for centuries to have my baby. Thanks to a successful campaign by Guardians of the sea, Mitsubishi's plan to desalinate Baja California waters has been abandoned. Thank you, Guardians. Thank you, Mitsubishi. No more ceasing seas.

As Tiger, my body is taut and tense as I pace back and forth in my tiny cell at the local zoo. It's 110 degrees and I can't get away from the sun. I'm thirsty! I have knocked over my water pan in my frenzy to escape the heat. Have they forgotten me? Maybe if I scream and leap from wall to wall, they'll hear me. Let me in! Open the door to the cool inside the building! Please get me out of the sun! Please, please, please!

Searing pain scorches my Calf shoulders as I am thrown down and roped tightly by a rodeo cowboy. In less than seven seconds! Clap your hands! Applaud everybody! Great job, man! You showed them who's the boss!

I smell the smell of my Skunk-ness. I thought I could cross a quiet country road safely at two in the morning. The glow of my eyes didn't protect me when a drunken kid driving his dad's pickup suddenly appeared out of nowhere and struck me broadside. He won the bet. He showed his friends that he could hit me hard enough to make my skin break open. I can still hear their laughter as the truck sped away. What's so funny?

We are Sheep moaning somewhere in Greece. We've been thrown alive onto a truck and stacked on top of each other. Our legs are broken, bruised and bleeding. No time to honor our sacrifice for someone's gyro sandwich.

Our Dolphin songs echo across hundreds of miles of ocean calling our families to join the feast. Come one, come all! Follow the trail of the Tuna fishing ships. We love the game of entrapment. Some of us win.

As Hawk, I feel the wind under my wings. I am soaring across open space searching for Mouse. Below me are bulldozers tearing away my food's habitat for another shopping mall. What's an espresso?

I hear my frantic barking. I am Dog caged in an animal shelter calling to my keepers. Where are they? Where's my family? What did I do? I'll never do it again, I promise!

I lay in bed trembling. The room is spinning. I am dizzy with my helplessness. Who am I? I don't know anymore. Then "they" appear as they always do. They catch me before I sink deeper into the dark of my darkness. Light appears and warms me. I hear them! I know I hear them. "It's all right, dear one. It's all right." It's the animals' turn to speak.

"We've been waiting for you to wake up. There is no separation from us. You are in charge. All you have to do is let go of fear. Trust yourself. Trust us. Accept the wonder of life as we do. We need you now."

A chill shimmies down my back. If I am to find the answer to my question, I must leap empty-handed into the unknown. I've been afraid to make any kind of leap because I don't know how to face the unknown. Not knowing what lies ahead has always frightened me. I'm ready now.

But where am I going?

ACT 2

SANCTUARY

THREE
The Question

THERE WAS NO TIME to think about what happened next. I don't know how long it took to get here. But where is here? I know I can leave whenever I want to. In the blink of an eye. The animals have been waiting for quite awhile. I was thrilled to see my Cat sitting among them. I picked him up and smothered his head with kisses. "Not in front of the others," he me-owed, squirming out of my arms. Good old Cat. Always acting tougher than he was.

One of the biggest Orangutans I've ever seen handed me a leaf filled with cool water. He silently pointed to a cushion of grass for me to sit on. I was about to thank him, but the animals' mood shifted the sweet moment into a sense of crisis. There would be no time to get acclimated.

Land animals and birds that live on every continent on Earth and in my own back yard sat silently watching me. I had a feeling countless others were in the forest and the sea beyond. No one feared me. I never felt so safe. Even with so many beings surrounding me, it didn't seem crowded. Prey and predator stood or sat side by side. Not one made a sound. Not a rustle of a feather could be heard.

I assumed they couldn't speak my language, but guessed they would get their message through to me somehow. Almost immediately, I began to get pictures of the animals' thoughts in my mind. I was shown scenes from prehistoric days when the other animals and first humans shared the bounty of the land, seas and skies. Over time, the relationship between humans and animals was severed when people took control of the Earth. Today the network of life is fragile. Worse, in jeopardy. The animals can no longer sit on the sidelines and do nothing. Humans are taking more than what they need from the lands and seas with alarming efficiency. Time has run out. It is now or never.

The animals had a theory. From their long association living among the featherless two-leggeds, they learned that something called "beliefs" cause great conflict among humans. The animals didn't understand why "beliefs" were so important to humans. They certainly didn't have any "beliefs" or want any. What do beliefs have to do with survival? They suspected that people's beliefs were the cause of the animals' problems.

So this is why I am here! The nightmares that haunted me about the plight of the other animals make sense now. I must have been hearing the animals' question psychically and made it mine! *What happened to the animal-human spiritual connection?*

The animals explained their daring plan to me. They intend to invite the very animal species that is destroying itself and taking every other animal along with it to a neutral place, where all points of view will be valued as credible solutions to their question. Their first step was to ask the Universe for help. From the moment of their plea, a small planet appeared somewhere out here in the cosmos. They call it *Sanctuary*. It will be the meeting place for all the animals, including humans. In this marvelous setting the other animals hope the answer to their question will be revealed.

Ambassadors were selected from the thousands of species living on Earth to set up residence here. Of the millions of insect species, the few that particularly affect human lives were given tickets to go. As Nature's caretakers, the animals immediately established balance and harmony in their new environment.

A deep voice boomed across Sanctuary. Startled, several birds scattered in the air then returned to their perches. I must have jumped two feet off my seat. Ignoring our reaction, Polar Bear opened the meeting. Her species is endangered and needs help now! Her habitat is disappearing. She is frightened by the sounds of gigantic sections of ice cliffs crashing into the ocean day and night. After hunting for sparse food, her daily swim to her home base is often more than one hundred and fifty miles across the Arctic water. Her young son couldn't make it yesterday. She's not sure she can make the swim if the ice floats further apart.

Arctic Tern confirmed Polar Bear's report and gave an account of the effects of the increasing warming of the Earth. Tern's tribe migrates thousands of miles from the Arctic to the Antarctic every year. "It's worse than you think. The melting is happening much faster than we can remember," he said.

Snow Goose concurred. "The warming is affecting Earth's ecology. Changing weather patterns make navigating the skies difficult for every bird species. Especially for those of us who travel long distances. Many cannot reach their breeding grounds."

The other migratory animals described the terror of being caught in increasingly massive storms, and how they barely escaped from the giant ocean waves crashing across the lands. Many cannot tolerate the unusually hot summers and harsh winters and simply die.

"Survival is becoming difficult for all life forms. In just a few years, the Arctic ice formations will be completely melted," Tern said sadly. "What will happen to our world then?"

The animals living in tropical rainforests spoke next. They couldn't understand why men are setting giant fires and using monster machines to destroy their habitats. During the rainy season, floods and landslides are a common occurrence. The forest animals are forced to live at the edge of territories where their tribes have lived for thousands of generations. They must constantly migrate to stay away from human-occupied lands.

Cow stepped in and apologized for his being a major cause of the forest destruction. Millions of his kind are placed on land that once were rainforests to graze until they are fat enough to be slaughtered. The shrinking global village has made it possible for the fast food industry to sell their flesh to large populations who have never heard of a hamburger. Until now.

Blue Whale emerged from the sea to remind us, "For decades, the United States military has been testing what humans call 'mid-frequency sonar' off the Hawaiian Islands and other locations throughout the globe. The ear-splitting sonar affects us and other marine mammals throughout the world's oceans," she moaned. "The high-intensity soundings blast my family with noise infinite times more intense than levels our bodies can tolerate, and cause our internal organs to hemorrhage. The sonar affects our hearing and we can't navigate, let alone care for our young. Deafened, hundreds of us drop to the sea floor and ultimately drown."

Before diving back into Sanctuary's sea, the great one asked, "The military knows that the sonar is killing us. Why do they continue testing when they already have the answers to whatever it is they seek?"

"Kaah!" Raven croaked in raspy voice, "We have no time to sit around and cry. I'm revered by the Native American Indians and hated by the American farmers. Millions of our Crow cousins have been killed along with us because the farmers are afraid we'll eat all their crops. As if we could! We take only what we need!" he said wiping his bill in disdain. "I've flown miles across lands without finding the borders where one crop begins and another crop ends. The human food garden has replaced our natural habitat. We can't find rodents and other foods we crave with shooters always at our backs."

"Caw!" Crow shouted. "What can we do? Where can we go? We birds have been on the Earth for several hundred million years in countless species of flying forms. We've earned our place by surviving everything dished out to us. Famines, storms, and ice ages. But we may not survive the Human Age. Some of us have moved to the cities to escape the shooters and find food wherever we can. Pigeons and Sea Gulls are living thousands of miles inland feeding on garbage dumps and begging on the streets. It breaks my heart to see that."

"Oorhh!" shouted Pigeon from a high branch. He dropped down onto a nearby rock as his mate landed at Snow Leopard's foot to accept a seed. "Speak for yourself, Crow! We pigeons have had a unique relationship with humans for thousands of years! They've just forgotten about us, that's all." Distracted, he cocked his head and flew to his life partner and began to strut around her. Bobbing his head, he cooed a love greeting. She clearly wasn't interested. Sighing, he returned to the rock and said, "There was a time when we had an important job serving them and in turn enjoyed their protection and company."

Raven hoo-cawed and said, "Yeah, *Squab*, you served them, all right! You were served to them!" Ignoring Raven, Pigeon continued, "We began working for humans thousands of years ago. We were quite good at delivering their messages to each other from one location to another. Some days we'd fly for hundreds of miles. We were respected, and well taken care of. Until 'they' invented the telegraph in the nineteenth century, our services were widely used around the world."

His chest puffed up as he added, "We are a courageous species. The most famous hero among us was a fellow pigeon named Cher Ami who was enlisted in the U.S. Army in 1918. With much of his body shot away, Cher Ami made it across enemy lines to deliver information that saved the lives of hundreds of soldiers!"

Pigeon's voice softened. "But you're right, Raven. Today we are being wiped out in the cities by 'pest control' operations. We're called *pests, 'flying rats!'* (Sorry, Rat.) We are forced to beg on the streets. Many of us rarely live through the year. Concrete can't grow seed-bearing plants."

His mate interrupted. "Honey, don't forget the good times! The humans are so (sounded like a coo) funny sometimes. I especially love Sundays in the fall. We have a front row seat watching their gods play games."

Games? Gods? I was so distracted by the fact they were speaking to each other in "human" language that I had to remind myself to pay more attention to what they were saying.

"Picture this," Dame Pigeon said. "The two-leggeds without wings construct giant coliseums all over the world where they worship their gods. Remember, dear? Last week, we flew over one of those structures built in a city called Denver. There they were! Hundreds of worshippers were dressed in orange and blue. Hundreds more were wearing red and white. The red and white ones had gathered in one section of a huge parking lot, and the orange and blues were in another. The red and whites hooted and howled at the orange and blues. The orange and blues howled back. Very funny!

"We guessed they were preparing for their worship service by sitting in the back of their cars eating and drinking. After the crowd satisfied their hunger and great thirst, they joined many more thousands entering the coliseum. We like this part of their ritual best because we can feast on the crumb mess they leave behind.

"From our view in the skies, the crowd seemed to become a

single flow of a strange orange and blue and red and white river. The river branched out as the blue and orange ones flowed one way, and the red and whites flowed in the opposite direction. Once seated, the minions quieted down in anticipation of their gods' arrival."

She eyed a particularly lovely nut someone had dropped. After gulping it down, she continued. "This is when it got exciting! Somewhere below the worshippers' seats, a door opened and many gods adorned in orange and blue charged onto the field! The thousands wearing the same colors stood up as one and praised their gods with a thunderous roar. It filled the air! I had to be careful or the winds from the sound would have knocked me out of the sky. Their prayer was a strange one. 'Go! Go! Win! Win!'"

Her partner fluttered to her side adding, "We still haven't figured out where they want their gods to 'go!' Then, the red and white's gods emerged from another side of the coliseum. They ran onto the field as their worshippers tried to outdo the orange and blue ones, yelling. '*Yay! Yaay! Go! Go! Goooo!!!*' By that time, every one of the thousands stood, stomped, swayed, waved signs and pompoms spilling beer on each other and every which way!" He laughed. "It's very funny watching humans get passionate about their deities. It's funny to us, but they don't seem to be laughing. We have a feeling they are out for blood."

Clearly excited, Dame Pigeon rose in the air and returned to the ground to interrupt her mate. "Then things got rough! An elliptical ball was thrown and caught by one of the orange and blue gods. All the gods raced toward each other crashing their hard heads together, pushing and grabbing necks, legs, and arms! Anything to knock the others down. We still haven't figured out what they were fighting about."

The Pigeons looked at each other. The look in their eyes reflected deep sadness. She said, "Go ahead, dear. Tell them the whole story." He nodded and continued. "We've seen these battles between the gods all over the world. In the Middle East worshippers of one religion have been fighting a deadly war with worshippers of another religion over their particular religion's doctrines for centuries. We must fly high to avoid the smoke from the fires. Too often we see children huddled in the rubble. Dead

Donkeys, Cats and Dogs lie on the ground close by. The game is hard on the young ones and the animals. What will happen to them?" He turned to his mate. His tears were choking him. Unable to continue, the life mates tenderly touched each other's beaks and flew off.

"Quork!" Raven muttered, "Listen! We could talk for years about human antics. We must go on. We can't give up!"

Lynx suggested that most impending disasters could be avoided if the human leaders would take action to prevent them.

Dog smiled wistfully at Lynx. "I wish it were that simple. You obviously haven't spent much time among humans," she said.

Lynx nodded. Her tribe spends their days avoiding humans. Long ago, Rabbit noticed that Lynx's cautious ways were fortunate for his family. Rabbit is Lynx's favorite food. Rabbit figured if his family settled into human habitats where Lynx won't go, they'd live longer. Maybe so.

Dog growled softly, "My species has sat at the feet of humans for over 32,000 years. We have lived among humans longer than any other animal has! We still haven't figured them out. We were the first to be invited to enter their sleep places as their friend, guardian and servant. In some parts of the world, we're still on their menus. Bon appétit!"

She paused to sip a little water from a nearby puddle and continued. "In ancient civilizations, especially old Egypt, many animal species were elevated to the status of gods and goddesses. Even insects were worshipped." Flies swarmed around Dog's ears buzzing, "Even the insects?" Apologizing for her insensitive remark, Dog brushed the buzzing ones away, and told them the animals appreciate them. They are an important link in the food chain. Satisfied, the little ones flew to Black Bear who was dipping his paws into a honey pot. There was plenty of the sweet sticky stuff to share. Bear didn't seem to mind. Not here in Sanctuary anyway.

I scratched several very itchy bites someone had given me last night and thought, "In this case, I am a link in one insect's food chain."

Dog began to pace. "As 'deities' (a position we did not ask for) humans worshipped and prayed to us to give them victory in battles, perform miracles, even provide them with food and gold. When we couldn't grant them the favors they expected, our 'divinity' took a deadly turn. People decided that human-like deities were the real gods and goddesses.

"The worshippers of the human-like gods-goddesses-God believed their gods got hungry as they did, and created blood sacrifice rituals to appease their deities' hunger. The humans figured why sacrifice a perfectly good human body when any other animal body would do? Since then, people have 'sacrificed' millions of cows, sheep, goats, dogs, and all kinds of animals to their gods."

Stopping to scratch her behind, Dog asked Flea to try to control himself. "Humans put a lot of stock in what they call their 'souls.' They worry about what happens to their 'souls' after they die. That's why they build all those grand structures where they can hold their religious ceremonies. They believe their gods will be pleased if they gather in large groups to chant and worship that which they don't understand." She paused to let her comments sink in. Many of the animals were unclear about why the humans would chant and worship something they don't understand when there are so many other things to do.

Dog explained, "Down through the ages, Dogs have been present in the great rooms with men and women who called themselves 'rulers.' We can't bring them to Sanctuary. Nothing would be accomplished with so many egos to contend with."

Tiger looked down at Shrew who was sitting between his legs. "What is an 'Ego?' Is 'Ego' edible?" Shrew replied, "Must be an animal we've never met."

After finishing a lovely roll in the grass, Dog made a suggestion that would change the animal and human spiritual connection forever. It was simple. "Why not ask the Universe to determine which humans should attend our meeting?" With that, Dog lay down and began her nap. "Wake me if you need any more advice about people. I'm an expert," she yawned.

After putting Tiger in charge of finding an "Ego" the animals did what Dog suggested and called upon the Universe for help. The great feline ran into the forest to find the new species. He returned days later and reported that he couldn't find such a creature. "Ego doesn't exist among the other animals," he said.

A sharp screech pierced the skies. Red Tail Hawk dove into the circle and delivered the news. "Our request has been granted! The Universe has assigned special people to travel to Sanctuary. It was explained to me that their unique involvement in animals' lives qualifies them to make the journey. They will somehow merge together in 'collectives' that will embody a few heroic figures called 'Universal Images.' The Universal Images will be able to shift into the physical appearance of the individuals contained within them," the great bird said nervously. "There could be hundreds of personas residing within each form!"

Hawk was exhausted. Before tucking his head into his wing to rest, he added, "It is our job to invite those Universal Images we think can best answer our question." Beaver dropped the branch she was dragging to the river. "How can that be? Has the Universe gone mad?"

Hawk raised his head to reply, "I'm not sure how it will happen. This is all I know." The animals began to get agitated. The idea of many humans dwelling within a few bodies was hard to imagine. Probably dangerous to them.

"Let me explain," Owl said. (Owl's wisdom is widely accepted among the animals and some humans.) The animals quieted. "Let's say one of the Universal Images will represent people whose life work is in something they call "Science." We will call that Universal Image "*Scientist.*" The Scientist will represent every scientist from past and present who has affected animal lives." Owl turned his head all the way around to his back to check out some annoying sounds. Two baby Squirrels stopped their play and hung their heads. Staring at the disrupters as only Owl can do, he remembered how tasty those bushy-tailed Squirrel kittens would be back on Earth.

Sighing, he continued. "We could assign another to be "*Cleric.*" Just think! Every religious leader who has influenced beliefs about animals as dictated by their god-goddess-God would coexist within one human form! Et cetera, et cetera." (The animals loved it when Owl spoke Latin.) Owl looked down at Dog. "Is that what you have in mind, Dog?" Dog, deep in sleep, was running after Cat who had entered her dream. Fully awake,

Cat was safe in the grasses stalking Butterfly. Owl ruffled his feathers and dug his beak into his chest. (Flea has been busy.)

"This could become confusing!" complained Blue Jay. "I'm already nervous just thinking about what might happen!"

Deer snorted and said, "You're always nervous, Jay! There's no turning back now. I think the plan will work once we get the hang of it. Let's get started! As we speak, many of my tribe are trapped behind fences set up for target practice by shooters who are not hungry."

Clearly upset, Elephant was swaying from side to side. She hadn't been able to bring herself to talk about Elephants' situation in the hands of men. Her distress ran deep. Many members of her tribe are going insane attacking villages and crops. They are even killing each other. Young male Elephants have been raping and killing Rhinoceroses in a number of reserves in African regions. Animal conservationists believe the reasons for the Elephants' insanity are pressures brought on by ivory poaching, environmental toxicity and the destruction of their habitat.

I wonder. Could there be a greater reason for the Elephants' madness? Every animal on Earth interacts with its own species, often over great distances. We humans must use mechanical devices to communicate with each other. Elephants have their own interspecies communication system without using plugs and sound boxes. Not too surprising since Elephant has been living on the Earth for at least fifty million years. Over countless generations, they've developed telepathic airwaves to 'talk' to each other across their own territories. Maybe they are capable of communicating to each other across continents, just as Whale is able to call other Whales over hundreds of miles of seas.

Could it be the Elephants know what is happening to their family members wherever they are on the Earth? Perhaps when circus Elephants are whipped in New York City, their cousins in Africa and Asia feel the blows. The common way of "taming" Elephant is to capture him when he is a baby, tie him to a post, and gore his legs deep. Bone deep. The excruciating pain quickly teaches the baby to submit and obey humans. Maybe the Elephants are furious because they cannot live out their life cycles in peace. They don't understand why some humans are so cruel to their kin. Perhaps they are in a state of madness because they realize they have a mere few years left to live on their own lands. There is no room on Earth for their species anymore.

I think mammals, birds, fish and insects are aware of their own species in similar ways. It's a matter of survival. My Cat always knew when another cat was nearby. His ears would perk up and he'd hunch down to disappear under a bush. Time stood still for him as he waited for that other Cat to appear from some hidden spot I never dreamed existed. Cats become aware of the presence of one of their own species before they sense the presence of another species. (Unless the other species is dangerous, or a possible snack.)

My Dog barks long before a strange Dog comes into sight. Birds appear to conduct their business solely for the sake of their own species. They seem to be oblivious or disinterested in the other animals walking below or sharing the skies with them. Sometimes one species crosses another species' line. One of my most predictable laughs in the spring is when a tiny Sparrow races into the sky to chase a hapless, almost-egg-stealing Crow doing his best to get away.

There's no doubt we human beings are first and foremost interested in our own survival. Could this be why we allow the gentle giants Polar Bear, Elephant, and Whale to survive on their own? We have our own problems.

The animals' discussion strengthened their determination to get to the root of the animal-human spiritual disconnection. They narrowed their list to ten Universal Images: *Scientist, Cleric, Philosopher, Sage, Skeptic, Teacher, Guardian, Change Maker, Healer, and (Animal) Communicator.* Turtle suggested the Universal Image of *Humanity* be invited to join the conference as an observer. "Humanity is the reason why we are here in the first place," she said.

The idea of Humanity joining their meeting in the form of a single being terrified the animals. After a heated discussion, they agreed to invite the Universal Image of Humanity to represent every human on Earth. Humanity would be forbidden to speak and not interfere with the proceedings in any way. Ever.

The animals would soon learn that people cannot (will not) be typecast whether they are contained within the forms of a few "Universal Images" or not.

PREPARATIONS FOR OUR GUESTS' arrival began in earnest. There was much to do. There's plenty of room for us all. Sanctuary has no borders. I've never walked its perimeters, and don't want to. I sense it is as deep as the soul and as wide. A river lazily ambles down from the hills, then picks up pace as it descends into the sea. In some places along its body, the waters gain momentum and turn into white foam rising and falling. It's a natural roller coaster. I love taking a ride on its rush into the crystal pure ocean. In this magical place I can breathe under the waters as easily as on land. Sometimes a water-dweller joins me. We explore the underwater caverns and race each other across the hills and valleys on the sea floor.

Strange reptiles, exotic birds, colorful insects and many species of fur-bearing ones from all-time sip from the fresh waters then disappear into the bush. I have seen creatures grazing and flying overhead that can only be described as otherworldly. Am I imagining them? Where do they come from? It's wonderful to be here!

From my field of vision I can see across the seas as far as I can imagine. The pale turquoise blue of the shallows blends into azure, flows into cyan, eases into the deep of Prussian blue, then merges into the dark mystery of black. The stars above reflect their beacons of light on the waters. I can't determine whether they are light years away or shining up from the deep.

I strain to see what lies way, way out there. The blackness of outer space and the deep black sea waters meld together to give the illusion that there is no discernable line of demarcation between the sea and the cosmic skies. They seem to be one and the same. I shiver wondering whether what I see is an optical trick or whether there is in truth no break between Sanctuary and the vast infinite of space.

Great bowers form a towering canopy above the ancient forest. The trees seem to be competing to be the first to reach the stars. Their branch roof opens to the ever-shifting skies. Light from the planets and stars cut through the dark of outer space illuminating Sanctuary perfectly. Sometimes I think I can see the entire Universe all at once. Last night I saw a star die. It went out with such a blast that I had spots in my eyes for several hours. It's true. I'm not on Earth anymore.

I wish I could share the sense of completeness the skies give me. Millions of galaxies spiral like puffs of smoke across the cosmos. A myriad of suns send out their light into the dark to give the illusion that the outer space is multi-dimensional. The contrast between the darkness and light is dazzling. Makes me think of the hall of mirrors I loved to explore in carnival fun houses as a child. I would lose myself in the game of finding my real image among the multiple reflections of me. Those halls of mirrors broadened my imagination, and taught me to recognize what is real and what isn't.

The awesome beauty of the cosmos washes away my dread of the unknown that seems to be the very essence of Sanctuary. I explore Sanctuary in ambivalence. Afraid of the mystery yet curious about what is to come.

For all its vastness, Sanctuary is more like an intimate friend. The air seems to breathe on its own. Sweet-smelling air. First baby breath air. The more I think about it, I'm sure Sanctuary is conscious of its beingness. Sanctuary anticipates every animal's thoughts without giving their thoughts a second thought. There is no doubt that Sanctuary can be trusted and that makes everything all right.

I can't help but wonder if the travelers, no matter how well they understand the purpose of their visit, would come to Sanctuary if they knew what was in store for them. They have signed up for the biggest task ever undertaken by animals and humans working together without the use of whips, chains or bars.

The animals are growing more restless every day. They are in a state of constant play and activity in anticipation of their guests' arrival. Gorilla is betting the answer to their question is not going to be found easily if at all. Dog and cat agree. Deer doesn't think it's possible. Pig is despondent. His relationship with humans is deadly. Horse gently nuzzles her foal, "Get up, little one. Time to move on to higher ground where you will be safe." Fresh warm breezes are waiting just within earshot to clear the air when needed.

And so we wait . . . we animals.

Four
Arrival

THEY'RE COMING! No one refused the animals' invitation. For some, the invitation seemed to be more of a challenge: *It is time for a universal shift in human consciousness, which reconnects humankind with the other animals – not only for the Earth's sake, but also for the evolution of the human soul.*

How could they resist the call? As the word spread among the chosen ones, they couldn't get here fast enough. We didn't have to send out a map or directions. They said they knew the way. For a few, the trip has taken centuries. I picture their light paths streaking across the cosmos as they pass through time and space to attend this historic conclave.

Upon each Universal Image's arrival, Sanctuary delivered a disturbing lesson. At first the visitors thought they hadn't traveled very far. Some imagined the trip was a dream. Others believed they had been transported to an undiscovered primordial forest on Earth. The awesome, unworldly terrain was familiar to them somehow. Smelling the delicious smells of the exotic plants and touching the soft petal of an unknown flower, they realized the trip was no dream. The sounds of bird songs and animal calls filled the air. Yet no living creature could be seen anywhere. Where were the sounds coming from?

Suddenly as if by signal, the sounds stopped. One by one, each visitor was enveloped in absolute, out-and-out, utter silence. The lush foliage of the forest became artificial, two-dimensional. Strange light illuminated the atmosphere. It was as if a dull gray curtain had been pulled across the skies. The profound silence smothered courage, raised heart-pounding fear and doubt. Where were the other animals? Where were the other travelers?

The sounds of the forest returned and their frightening ordeal ended when each being realized he and she must trust themselves and trust their intention if they were to remain here. When they finally gathered together as a group, they told a remarkably similar story. It was as if they were reading from the same script.

Scientist was first to speak. "*I thought I was alone in this strange place. I could hear the animals around me but couldn't find one! Not even a Gnat. I assumed the animals were shy or playing a game with me, so I didn't speak. I just walked softly, listening to their din. Then all sounds stopped. I thought I'd gone deaf! Never was a silence as silent as this silence.*"

Teacher added, "*I couldn't hear my own footsteps. That really made me nervous. I sat down on a rock and waited for someone to come along. Once I caught my breath, I sensed the animals were watching me. I couldn't speak or move for a long time. I experienced that familiar darkness in my head that always comes over me when I am in doubt. I hadn't anticipated fear would be in Sanctuary. The unknown became terrifying.*"

"Then," Cleric said, "*it came to me that the silence was some sort of a test. It was a test of my trust in my decision to come. If I disappointed the animals, I would be disappointed in me. As soon as I realized this, I forgot what I was so afraid of. With that, birds reappeared on the branches and in the skies. Several Butterflies landed on my outstretched hand!*"

Philosopher continued, "*It was marvelous! I spotted Giraffe peering at me across tall flowers. Zebra walked into the clearing and playfully nuzzled me. Lion emerged from the bush and sat down at my side. I hesitated and touched his mane. He began to purr. The leaves on the trees and the grasses rustled as if a wind had brought them back to life. Then I saw you and another and another wandering the forest looking as dazed as I was. You can imagine my relief!*"

Change Maker said, "*For a moment I thought I'd landed on an empty stage of a theater and an audience was somewhere out there watching my every move. It was eerie.*" She laughed. "*Here we are in a galaxy far, far away, and we've brought our emotional baggage with us!*"

Once they knew they were safe, the newcomers decided to go their separate ways to explore their new surroundings. There would be plenty of time to get acquainted later. The pure water from the streams, sweet nectar from giant flowers that grew everywhere, wild fruits, exotic vegetables and nuts nourished them. No one went hungry. No one ate another.

We had a wonderful time swimming under the sea. Even the Universal Image of Philosopher, who usually appeared to us as an elder, was able to dive deep into Sanctuary's magical waters and explore without cumbersome equipment strapped to his back.

Sea creatures of every conceivable size and color tickled us with their fins and gently nibbled us. It was grand! The Dolphins and Whales communicated their histories and adventures in musical tone. We were touched by their friendliness.

We jogged through the woods with ease, always accompanied by an animal that slowed down to meet our pace. The animals' sensitivity toward our physical inability to move easily in the thick bush or climb over rocks and through tall grasses revealed their cooperative nature. If one got tired, Elephant appeared and lowered her trunk and gently elevated the human to her head.

The larger animals stayed close to give a ride if one needed it. I frequently hitched a ride on the shoulders of Grizzly Bear. I have never felt so safe as I was nestling in her sweet smelling fur! Teacher said it best. "How many of us would do the same for the animals? How many of us would slow down to move at their pace?"

Colorful birds followed us everywhere. Sometimes they teased us by gently brushing their wings on our cheeks. Often they'd deliver a flower or a bit of fruit. I was in awe of the smaller birds' athletic prowess as they darted between close-knit branches. They'd soar above the canopy, then free fall to float at our shoulder height to chatter in our ears. Parrot explained that if we listened carefully we'd hear messages in their chatter. Messages delivered with such rapidity that our ears couldn't adjust to what they were saying. Yet. We later learned their songs were mostly about being in this wondrous, safe place.

At the end of the days, most of the group slept under the tree canopy in individual sleeping pods made out of giant leaves. A few of us constructed simple pulleys and suspended our pods from thick vines that grew to great heights on the trees. It was easy to raise and lower our pods at will and well worth the effort. The view from on high was breathtaking.

CR

THIS MORNING AT THE FIRST SIGN OF LIGHT, I began my daily run. This time I chose a path I'd never taken before. Filled with energy, I fairly flew for about an hour until I encountered a giant twisted tree with branches heading every which way. It grew smack dab in the middle of where I was going. I almost turned back to where I'd been, but my sense of adventure got the better of me. I decided to go on regardless the obstacle in front of me. After trying to walk around the humongous plant, I realized the only way I could get to the other side would be to climb up through its branches. It wasn't easy.

The more I struggled to break through, the tree would counter by growing more branches. I slowly made my way through its thick foliage until I found an opening. I pulled myself out, but caught my shoestring on a twig and fell on my knee. As I sat on the ground hugging my bruises and feeling sorry for myself, a shiny blue rock caught my eye. It was a little insignificant pebble hardly worth noticing. When I picked the stone up, a light shot out of an opening it had been covering. Its beam rose above the forest canopy and linked Sanctuary with the skies. Curiosity won over caution, and I peeked into the hole. In an instant the orifice widened, the ground gave way, and I tumbled into the void.

My fall couldn't have been more than seconds, but it seemed to be hours as I fell toward the source of the light. My fall suddenly slowed until I found myself floating under the ceiling of an enormous cave. Then I saw something that made me gasp. Millions of creatures were clinging to the walls of the cave so tightly together that they appeared to be one shimmering body. The massive crowd pulsated as they slowly moved in unison along the walls. As they moved, the creatures' bodies shifted into colors I'd never seen on Earth. The colors were the same colors of the galaxies and solar systems I passed on my trip to Sanctuary.

Moving in closer, I recognized them. Countless transparent, light-filled Bats were clinging to the cave wall and each other! Their glow lit the cave so brightly that I could see a valley of preternatural crystal formations that seemed to stretch for miles. A vast, calm lake mirrored fantastical crystal rock shapes that hung from the cave ceiling and rose up from the ground. The light emanating from the Bats echoed into the inner core of the crystalline cave walls, beamed through the giant formations, and crossed the cave rooms into the lake waters. The Bats, the cave, and the lake became interconnected in a bizarre network of light. The effect was much like a web of lasers spun by a remarkable Spider.

As if by signal the Bats broke away from the cave walls and formed a swarm that flew right at me! I covered my face fearing the worst! To my amazement they passed my shaking body, and in unison shot straight up. Thousands swirled into a grand spiral that rose to the heights of the cave then dropped effortlessly to skim the ground. It was a dance and I was invited to join. In this magical place, I could fly! We played for hours hiding in and out among the giant crystal formations. As we flew over the lake again and again, the waters began to glow, then filled with our light. The waters were so brightly lit I could see into their depths. I dropped out of the crowd to get a better look.

After a bit of slipping and sliding, I was able to climb onto a giant crystal rock and peer into the lake. I recalled looking out of an airplane window from six miles up to see the Earth's surface reduced to lines and craggy bumps. At that height, the Earth becomes a fabric of patterns and textures. I lost myself in the wonder of the water depths. To my amazement, I could see the same kind of patterns and textures at the bottom of the lake. Could the lake be miles deep? I shuddered, slid off the rock, and landed on my poor knee.

In a moment I was back where I started under the fallen tree still hugging my knee. What happened? Why was I back? I reached into my pocket. The stone was still there. It warmed my hand and comforted me. I had many questions but no one was around to hear them. Frantically, I dug up the earth, pulled out roots, and picked up every little rock in the area. The hole had disappeared.

When I finally looked up from my digging, the troublesome tree had shriveled into a round ball of thin branches. Had the tree always been a tumbleweed? I tried to touch it. Not fast enough. A sudden breeze tossed it into the forest. No tree. No bush. No hole. It was over. Somehow I found my way back to camp. Exhausted, I returned to my sleeping pod. As soon as my head sunk into my soft leaf pillow I was enveloped in a disturbing dream.

I am in a lightless cave filled with the stench of Bat crap. Listening to the animals' contented mutterings after a long night of feeding on insects, I feel at ease among these amazing animals. After living on the Earth for over 50 million years, Bats are evolutionarily advanced creatures. It took many of those years for Bats to discover that living in caves in the dankest of circumstances was safest for their species. They built their underground cities by clinging together on top and beneath each other in some sort of dysfunctional familial way. Most Bats can't make it without the crowd.

On the cave floor millions of flesh-eating beetles and other carnivorous critters are waiting to enjoy a good meal from the droppings of their hosts. Sometimes a young Bat slips from her nursery and falls into the mess. Unless she can immediately crawl up the slimy cave wall to a safe crevice, she is a fast food meal for the many below. A first-time mother's cry echoes through the chamber as her baby falls. It's a brief cry. There will be more little ones coming along. Next time, she'll be more careful with her charge. If she remembers next time. Some people despise and are repulsed by Bats until they learn how the bat kingdom balances Nature so neatly. Without the bats' nightly forays, insects would overcome the land.

We have much in common. They're mammals. I'm a mammal. Their cave is their shelter. It's mine too. They don't seem to know or care that I'm hanging from the ceiling of their cave wrapped in a cocoon of my own making. I'm busy spitting out the sticky goo of memories about my mistakes, regrets and shame. The goo forms layers and layers on the cocoon walls to protect my long-suffering ego who has been busy making sure I criticize and despise myself throughout lifetime after lifetime for being too fat, not pretty enough, not smart enough, not rich enough, not good enough. Not, not, not! Spit, spit, spit! If I fall down into the mess below, it will be my own doing. As long as I can, I will hold on.

My cocoon is heavy. I'm glad to be inside this solitary space. But then I've had lifetimes to keep my cocoon securely attached to the cave ceiling. I wonder how wide and long my cocoon is. I can easily break through its walls. It wouldn't be hard to open a passage and be free. But I can't. Not just now. Not yet. Spit, spit,

spit.

A conch shell tone filled the air and bounced off the cliff walls. The call to gather came just in time. My sleeping pod started to sway, then tossed me up and down. I woke up shaking. What did my dream mean? All I knew was I didn't want to go back to either of those caves.

What other mysteries will be revealed in Sanctuary? Over breakfast, I was relieved to hear the others had some morning adventures of their own. Like mine, their experiences related to their passions as well as their fears. I reached into my pocket and was pleased to find the pebble still there. I'll look at it later.

Sanctuary is permeating every aspect of our existence by revealing our past lifetimes to us when we least expect it. Someone said it perfectly. "As I visit one of my lifetimes, I am able to connect another dot mapping my soul."

Scientist recalled a lifetime eons ago in Atlantis. He cloned other animals into human beings and vice versa. "Scientists have always challenged Nature with no regrets," he said. "It's what we do."

Cleric was surprised that he was a giant Horsefly grown fat eating Dinosaur dung.

As Cat, wrapped in mummy cloth, Communicator was buried alongside his mistress.

Teacher reported sitting under a Bodhi tree among a throng of people. "We were listening to a man called Buddha. We didn't know who he was, but we knew the truth when we heard it," she said.

Sage was Bear living in an undiscovered, pristine forest giving birth to her cubs. No humans were around for hundreds of miles to interfere with their glorious life span (yet).

Diseased and freezing cold in a prison cell, Philosopher was chained to a wall for the rest of his lifetime for stealing a hunk of bread. Rats were his only companions. His mother turned him in for a coin. She had other mouths to feed.

Near a hill called Tor, a group of people in robes, their faces unrecognizable in the shadows of candles, solemnly push a giant boulder into the opening of a small cave where Guardian sits. He must prove he is worthy to become a Druid priest and dies a horrible, suffocating death taking some sort of test of his resolve.

It takes many lifetimes for his soul to stop the testing.

Hidden in a cave, Change Maker holds her beloved in her arms. He is mortally wounded from a battle he cannot fight anymore. Losing him will tear her soul from her body for centuries.

I hid in shame for hours when I recalled my warrior nature. My sword was bloodied after cutting off the nose of an enemy who denied my dogma and dared to have one of his own. I've lived lifetimes cutting off those who weren't like me. Always ready to kill to defend my truth, I've blasted across lifetime after lifetime devoted to my rulers, the emperors, pharaohs and chiefs of my tribes. I crossed the infinite of time brawling over some cause or another. Murderous, idealistic, angry, afraid, I judged and destroyed anyone who disagreed with me.

Then I became Eagle soaring across a Himalayan mountain peak. As I merged into the body of a monk meditating in his rock shelter, I realized who I really am. In another moment I forgot what happened.

On this particular day, our journey is about to take a hard turn.

FIVE
Getting Acquainted

T HE GROUP HAS GATHERED under the galactic skies. A fire crackles in a rock pit we've built in the center of the clearing. Not that we need a fire. Sanctuary's moderate climate suits us. It's taken days for me to get used to seeing personas of remarkable people emerge from their Universal forms to talk. When a persona emerges, he and she temporarily embody their Universal Image and "become" the speaker. It's unnerving. For me anyway. The others have no problem with the shifts.

It is the evening before the first day of our conference. The Universal Image of Humanity sits fondling a golden cord tied around her waist. Like the Chameleon, she becomes invisible if she leans against a rock or sits in the grasses. She came to Sanctuary as an observer but immediately became the observed. At first, some of us were uncomfortable when her body shifted back and forth, first as a woman, then as a man, and then back again. We would never see her as the same person twice during our entire visit here.

One of Humanity's physical features is most fascinating. Her skin is the color of amber and as translucent. One can usually determine what she is thinking by observing the flow of energy under the skin of those ever-changing faces. I wonder if our stares (no matter how subtle we try to be) annoy her.

The animals are adamant about keeping Humanity out of the conference proceedings. Most of them hoped she wouldn't show up at all. I understand their concern. She represents the collective of the entire human psyche. All seven billion of us. The animals aren't ready to face the true nature of human thought. When she arrived, many animals withdrew and hid in the forest fearing the worst. They know she has the power to be destructive. For certain, she is the most dangerous of all the animals.

As it is turning out, Humanity is enthralled with herself embodied in the other Universal Images and spends her days observing herself within them. The animals returned to the circle when they realized she had no intention of disrupting the meetings. The animals would soon learn that Humanity is incapable of staying out of anyone's business, and that would include the Universe's.

Tonight, all is gloriously peaceful. The thousands of galaxies swirling in the cosmos give me the feeling we are in some sort of multi-dimensional time warp. Every moment we're here, we are experiencing all the time that ever was, is and will be. And at the same "time," there is no time at all.

Healer and Communicator arrived together and seated themselves on large pillows stuffed with fragrant grasses and flower petals. In Sanctuary, when one thinks about something she and he wants or needs, it appears. Someone must have envisioned comfortable seating. Healer sat next to Scientist. She stared into the fire deep in her own thoughts.

Skeptic sits separate from us on the edge of the circle. Head down, he is taking copious notes. Skeptic soon observed that whenever he opens his mouth to speak, the canines growl and the smaller animals skitter away. Whenever he looks directly into an animal's eyes, all chatter and bird song stops. The animals' hostile response to his every move doesn't bother this odd fellow. In fact, he finds it amusing.

Yesterday, Skeptic questioned the primary rule we were to abide while we are here: There will be no dissension in Sanctuary. The visitors clearly understood why. By keeping the dialogue free of individual bias, all points of view will be accepted as viable information in our search for the answer to the animals' question. When he was reminded of the rule, Skeptic shouted, "Ridiculous! I will leave in the morning!"

Guardian said softly, "No, sir, you may not leave Sanctuary. When we do leave, we will leave together. You hold some of the answers to the animals' question. Your presence is required."

"Then I am a prisoner?" Skeptic whined.

Guardian replied, "You are free to roam anywhere you want

in Sanctuary. Once you have made your contribution to the discussion, you may leave. Besides, we hope you will honor us by sharing your ideas about the other animals' role in religion, philosophy and science."

I couldn't help but imagine Skeptic as a large, aggravated Rooster. Even his hair and clothing ruffled when he spoke. Curiosity got the best of him. He wondered which of his insights were most interesting to the group. He enjoyed a lively debate and was confident he could prove to us that the other animals have no souls. His "feathers" seemed to smooth, and he continued writing in his journal.

This evening, a persona emerged from the Universal Image of Scientist. He said, "Today, I felt as if I were in the Brazilian rainforest. The day has passed delightfully . . ." The small group conversations stopped. We turned to see Charles Darwin who had not revealed himself to us until this moment! For over one hundred years, few in the scientific world have questioned the great Naturalist's theory that every animal species evolved over time from one common ancestor. His theory ultimately turned scientific and religious beliefs of his day upside down, and has since raised complex questions about life in the Universe itself.

Many of today's religious thinkers, including the pope, view Darwin's scientific discoveries to be possible. They find his discoveries to be compatible to the story of the Creation found in their sacred texts. The exception would be the religions' fundamentalists who believe that questioning the original Creation story as told in their holy books is dangerous to their souls.

A golden galaxy disappeared on the horizon as Sanctuary revolved into what we began to mark as night. A new image of Scientist emerged. We recognized him to be one of the most provocative biologists and parapsychologists of the twenty-first century. Rupert Sheldrake has written extensively about his premise that everything in the Universe is alive with its own inherent memory. His view is gaining momentum as new scientists find his theory probable. He became one of my heroes when I learned he used real life examples of the psychic relationship between owners and their dogs in his book, *Dogs Who Know When Their Owners Come Home.*

Cat is lying on his back close to the image of Dr. Sheldrake. His loud purring doesn't disturb the Fireflies dancing among us. The Scientist stretched his lanky form and reached to stroke Cat and said, "When we look at the stars, we can consider the possibility not only that some may have planets around them with living beings on them (which I think very probable) but also that the very stars themselves may have a kind of life, intelligence, or spirit." The group excitedly leaned in to respond.

Just when things were getting interesting, I reluctantly excused myself from the circle. You see, the animals have asked me to facilitate this great convergence. If the many personas contained within the other Universal Image forms are as complex as Scientist's, I'd better prepare for our first assembly. It's time to face the animals' question.

Can't sleep. The encampment is quiet. Normally I love sleep time. I float into sweet dreams listening to the nocturnal animals calling to each other throughout the forest. This night, I can't quiet my agitated mind. Thoughts keep pouring in. Mostly "*What If's.*" What if the group raises conflicting questions that I can't mediate? What if the animals are disappointed with the way I conduct the meeting? Maybe I'll get sleepy if I take a walk in the moons' light. I lowered my pod from the treetop and crawled out into the lush grasses.

The full moons provided just enough light for me to find a basket of my favorite fruits at my pod entrance. I chose a lovely fruit and took a big bite. Its flavor was unworldly delicious. Little Monkey hopped onto my shoulder and began to search my hair for whatever he was looking for. I gently patted his back. He wrapped a thin arm around my neck and pressed his head against my cheek. His loving gesture quickened my heart.

Looking across the clearing, I noticed one of the pods on the ground was glowing. Good! Someone else is awake. Sure could use a bit of company right now. When I stood up, the tiny Marmoset protested with a short squeak and cried, "I thought I was good company!" and disappeared into the night. "Sorry, dear one," I called softly. "Come back tomorrow and we'll play!"

I walked over to the pod hoping to be invited in for a chat. Maybe this great being can explain to me how s/he can physically change into so many bodies. As I approached, the light within the pod brightened until it poured out of the pod entry and filled a good portion of the grass field outside. I began to doubt whether I should disturb the Universal Image. I turned around to go back to my pod, but couldn't control my curiosity and peeked inside the entry. What in the world?

Several amorphous, translucent forms were merging into one body. In moments, they separated from the one body to become dozens of shapes of human beings. I could see their bodies casting shadows through the pod walls! Then as if in a slow-moving dance, the many returned to become one being again. Wait! I think it is Scientist! What should I do now? I had just stumbled onto something I should never have witnessed! I backed away from the glow, tripped and twisted my ankle and limped-ran to my pod still resting on the forest floor. I pulled the vine with all my might. When my pod reached the safety of the treetop, I dove into my bed and pulled the covers over my head.

Guess I am sleepy after all . . .

Six
Keeper's Story

ON THIS GLORIOUS MORNING, the trees seem to be standing straighter. Many kinds of birds have filled the branches. Their symphonic song echoes throughout the forest. The flowers have filled the air with an intoxicating fragrance. The blues of the Sea have been replaced by an unexpected spectrum of colors. I felt a catch in my throat as I approached the circle. The animals have cleaned and preened themselves. Many have been waiting in the clearing before dawn. I am deeply touched by how proudly they sit. This is their day! The first official day of our conference is about to begin!

We formed our circle. Dozens of animal species sat among us. The larger animals stood close by. Elephant stayed on a hill to watch over her baby grazing below. When Elephant was elected by her tribe to represent elephants everywhere, she didn't know she was pregnant. We welcomed the next generation of her species. Horse's foal has grown into a handsome Colt. We weren't sure if there were other females carrying. Didn't matter. There's plenty of room in Sanctuary.

A shout broke the air. "Listen!" Teacher said. "Someone is calling for help!" Help in Sanctuary? Who could possibly be in trouble in Sanctuary? Off in the distance, the Raptors were flying in circle formation. Hyena left immediately to check it out.

We found him soaking in a pond surrounded by gigantic flowers at least nine feet tall! We thought they were trees but when we looked up their stalks each had produced one magnificent red bloom. I was transfixed by the sight.

"You must be Keeper," I say. "We've been waiting for you! Where have you been?"

He murmured softly, "I can't get clean." His eyes were red. He's been crying. "I feel so dirty! I haven't had a real bath for years! Then that camel ride through the desert covered me with more grime." His voice wandered off. "Let me stay in the water a little longer?"

Camel? Desert? The Keeper must be talking about the Zone just east of Sanctuary. Few have attempted to enter Zone. Fewer returned. It's a territory I have yet to explore. It is said the beings that live there can swim in its thick atmosphere and easily walk on its gelatinous surface. Light from some unknown source reflects one color. Red. In Zone, the skies, the ground, the waters and the life forms appear to be hundreds of shades of red. Somewhere in the back of my mind I know the source of the light. I just can't remember where.

The mountains have been worn down from the ages. They are reduced to strange twisted formations frozen into shapes resembling a tribal dance of giants. The earth rolls and undulates like a sea bottom without the sea. I've heard that walking on Zone's surface is much like walking on a waterbed or climbing a sand dune. Deep crevices pocket the land. Fathoms deep, they appear unexpectedly and close the moment one approaches them. I know those crevices. They are in the deepest recesses of my darkest dreams. Vivid during my sleep time, they disappear when I gratefully wake up.

I don't avoid Zone out of fear because I know I'm as safe there as I am wherever I am in Sanctuary. It's just that I have a feeling I'd have a difficult time breathing if I tried to cross its borders. It must be that soupy, stinking air that hangs over it. When I'm ready, I'll explore Zone further. I don't know when. Nor do I care when.

"I must have taken a wrong turn on the path I thought would lead me to Sanctuary," Keeper said, staring through me. It was as if he were talking to himself. "When I arrived, I saw a strange red light above the horizon. I thought it was Sanctuary! As I ran toward it, the light faded into an impenetrable mist. The path split into two roads right before my eyes. One road was covered with a thicket of dead, entangled vines. The other was smooth and paved with gold. I was forced to choose my own way. I chose the one paved with gold. Wouldn't you?

"For the first few hours, my steps became lighter and lighter until I swear I was walking inches above the ground. I moved along the path for days. Still no Sanctuary. Finally giving up, I turned around to go back to where I started, but some one or some thing blocked my retreat. I was forced to keep going where I was heading. There was no way I could leave the path I'd chosen."

Keeper paused to catch his breath. "As I walked along, I was pulled into what I am sure was another dimension. I can't explain it." His eyes opened wide in fear as he continued his story. "I thought I was going through some sort of initiation into Sanctuary, so I went along with it. I blindly walked for what seemed to be several more miles when suddenly the ground opened up and I fell into a deep pit!" The words were pouring out of Keeper now. "Can you believe it? I've been held captive in a hole in the ground for God knows how long! There was no way I could escape!" He almost laughed. I shivered.

"I couldn't see another living soul from my vantage point although I knew a lot of activity was going on. There was a lot of scurrying of footsteps moving above me throughout the day. I imagined great crowds coming and going. I heard howls from creatures I couldn't identify. For days, I laid on the ground in a state of terror. Sometimes a bird would fly overhead. I can't tell you how much I enjoyed seeing the birds soaring free out there. They'd arrive early morning and be gone at dusk. Then I'd be left alone again. So alone.

"I couldn't understand why they kept me in total isolation. Didn't they notice I am an intelligent being? I shouted my name and talked to them every day just to hear my own voice. I missed my family terribly. It took weeks to acclimate to the loneliness. I could almost taste my empty, boring days."

Cupping his hands, he filled them with water and drank thirstily. "My captors were primates, I'm sure of that. Hairy hands delivered fruit and some god-awful pellets through a portal they slid open in the side of the pit. When I became sick, they somehow knew. I didn't like them entering my 'home.' They'd have to sedate me before they could carry me to a room with bright lights. I'd find myself strapped to a steel table. No matter how hard I struggled, I couldn't break free. They never spoke directly to me."

He was growing more and more agitated, but was determined

to tell his story. "They wore surgical caps and masks and spoke to each other all the while poking and prodding me. I got a feeling that my captors were sympathetic to me but at the same time were disinterested in whom I was. Sometimes they'd stick the biggest hypodermic needle I'd ever seen into my belly or butt. The next thing I knew I was back in the pit. Sore, but feeling better."

His voice dropped so low that we had to lean forward to hear him. "The walls of the pit were rock. There was nothing soft where I could comfortably lay my head. I had the eeriest feeling I was constantly being watched during the day. At night, I'd search that dark red sky for stars, the moon. Anything to provide a clue where I was. Thank goodness there was a small cave carved into the wall of the pit. I could crawl into it when that red sun got unbearable or when it rained that awful red rain.

"Yesterday as if by magic, the pit fell away. Reminded me of a stage set being broken down after the last performance of a play. I was out! I was free! I think my captors wanted me to tell you what happened for reasons I have yet to figure out. It'll come to me. Amazingly, a little camel was grazing just outside the rubble that once was my prison. He was waiting for me, I think. I could easily mount him. This surprised me since I can't (won't) ride a Horse, let alone a Camel. I barely had settled on his hump when he took off at a full speed run. We flew like the wind. A bit bumpy, our trip across the Zone took just a moment. I was free!"

He stopped his story as quickly as he had begun. He seemed to be distracted by his own words. I tossed a white robe to him. He pulled the robe over his head and emerged from the pond. The robe was way too big for his small frame, but he wrapped it around his shivering body as if he'd worn it all his life. "The air here is just perfect!" he shouted. "The robe feels wonderful on my skin. Maybe none of this happened. Maybe it was some sort of dream. I'm OK now. Let's go!"

Those who had stayed behind in the circle jumped up from their seats and greeted the Keeper warmly. No one found it unusual that he remained outside of the Universal Image of Scientist for most of our stay in Sanctuary. The circle is expanding, yet we feel the same intimacy one feels when talking to a few good friends. Keeper stretched and sat on the ground.

Gibbon dropped from a tree and started to put her arms

around him, but quickly withdrew her hug and jumped out of the way. She saw what was coming before we did. We couldn't believe our eyes! Bars rose up from the ground and formed a cage around Keeper, giving him just inches to move. The bars were so high that we couldn't see where they ended. Someone remarked, "He is locked in an enclosure of his own making." Keeper smiled, "This often happens when I go somewhere. Pay no attention. I'm fine, really.

Like the Turtle, I bring my house with me."

SEVEN
Opening Day

THE KEEPER'S HARROWING EXPERIENCE was a wake-up call. We've had some exciting adventures here in Sanctuary, but Keeper's story reminded us that the "holiday" is over. Someone said, "Maybe by discovering what happened to the animal-human spiritual connection, we'll be able to understand what happened to our own place in Nature." Skeptic scoffed, "Our place in Nature? What does that mean? I know my place and it's above the other animals!"

As much as he tries to rile us, the group remains in a state of calm acceptance. This is frustrating for the Skeptic. He wants more than ever to return to the Earth in his times where he tells us he "belongs."

Some think the answer to the question is shrouded in mystery and should never be found. Others think the answer is right before our very eyes if we opened our minds. Regardless the answer, every persona within the Universal Images (well, almost every persona) sincerely wants to restore the spiritual connection between human beings and other animal species. It's time to begin.

As if by signal, we closed our eyes. In a short moment, we were immersed in the same heavy silence the group endured the first day of their arrival. Air held wind. Sea ceased movement and became a vast mirror reflecting the stars above and below. The galaxies appeared to grow still. This time, the group welcomed the silence. It disturbed me. Guess I will never forget growing up on the streets of Chicago. We learned at a young age to look over our shoulders wherever we were. Trusting the Universe requires practice.

A faint hum filled the air. "*Ommm!*" It was hard to tell where the sound was coming from. It seemed to come from nowhere in particular. I opened one eye a slit to see a solitary Bighorn Sheep standing on a cliff. Head raised high he exclaimed, "*Ommm!*" His sounding reverberated across Sanctuary. A blue fog slowly rose around him. He had entered that special state of consciousness that happens when one is in deep meditation. I opened both my eyes in time to see the great Sheep disappear into the mist chanting as he faded out of sight.

Someone (I think it was Gorilla) held onto the sound and kept it going. The other animals joined in. High pitch and low, it was one singular glorious note. Sparrow struggled to stay with the one note. It wasn't his song style, but it didn't matter. His chirping became a staccato "*Om! Om! Om!*" Lion rolled on his back, and offered the lowest of low "*Omm*" out of his belly. Bees swirled around us in harmonious chord.

A human Image joined in counterpoint, and then another until every human in the gathering, including a very confused Skeptic, joined the chant. "*Ommmm!*" The forest and cliffs echoed the sound. No chorus anywhere anytime on Earth or in the Cosmos for that matter, has produced a sound like our sound. I am sure of it. Our sound was extraordinary. We had become one voice. It was unanimous. A great start to an uncertain day.

My breathing began to speed up, then stopped. I was paralyzed. Who am I to facilitate this meeting? How did I get here in the first place? Somebody (anybody) get me out of here! Owl revealed himself on a branch above me. His eyes filled with encouragement. Cat stepped into the circle and gently wrapped his tail around my ankle in an attempt to comfort me. I was frozen. Vole jumped onto my shoulder and whispered, "Begin! The humans are here to work with us. They are not going to bite your head off. Tiger is going to do the biting if you don't get started!" I had to laugh and remembered our greater purpose. This is not the time for my ego to swallow me up in self-consciousness.

Change Maker smiled at me and nodded her encouragement. She stood and entered the circle. Without saying a word, her body began to shift into the images of a few people that changed the world. First to appear was a man who led a revolution causing the fall of the Czar system in Russia. Vladimir Lenin's ideas for creating a better society were interpreted by self-proclaimed autocrats to mean change requires the suffering and death of millions. His face was lined with the anguish of regret. Lenin's body became a blur and he disappeared all together.

A thin man wrapped in simple white cloth stood in his place. We easily recognized Mohandas Gandhi who convinced millions in India to resist tyranny by practicing non-violence. The Indian people's widespread observance of "ahimsa" toward British rule inspired worldwide respect for what they endured to become free. After years of struggle, they won their country's independence.

Another transformation, and a very old, very small woman in the habit of a nun stood before us. Mother Teresa, born Agnesë Gonxhe Bojaxhiu, was a Catholic nun of Albanian origin who founded the Missionaries of Charity to serve the lower castes of India. Mother Teresa and her small religious order selflessly nurtured thousands of diseased and dying poor who were kept hidden away from the tourists. Her compassion over the plight of these unfortunate people as well as her personal appeals, moved people around the world to contribute to her work. After she died in 1997, public awareness dimmed and India's poor continue to suffer hidden away from view. It was painful to look into her eyes. The good nun became encompassed in light, then disappeared.

In her place stood the image of Jane Goodall. With her long gray hair tied back into a ponytail, we recognized the renowned Change Maker. She lived for many years in the jungles of Gombe Park in Tanzania to document the similarities of chimpanzees to humans. Jane Goodall travels tirelessly to convince the world community that chimpanzees (and every free species) have the right to live safely in the wild. (It's a matter of survival for us all.)

Another shift and Change Maker became the familiar image of a renowned twenty-first century activist and peacemaker. She had clearly demonstrated to the group that they too could influence societal change on Earth. We sat quietly for several minutes. I waited until my heartbeat quieted. This is the time that has been waiting for us to catch up with it. Inspired by Change Maker's courage, I was ready to begin.

I rose from my seat and slowly entered the center of the circle. "Thank you for coming on such short notice," I said. Philosopher grinned. Short notice? His trip has taken twenty-four centuries. I looked into his eyes and my agitation returned. As much as I have tried, I cannot get his stories out of my mind.

The other evening over the supper table, Philosopher and Cleric told us about their encounter en route to Sanctuary. Aristotle, the fourth century BCE Philosopher, met up with (Saint) Thomas Aquinas, a most influential priest of the thirteenth century Roman Catholic Church. Thomas is renowned for his theology of natural law. The priest agreed with Aristotle's theory that an animal's brain size determined its soul's size. So much so that he expanded the Philosopher's premise, and declared that an animal's soul size determined that animal's rank in God's plan. His view remains in the Church doctrines, and is found in the Catechism today.

At first, Aristotle was pleased that most other Christian churches' doctrines adopted his theory too. His pleasure grew dark when he read the Bible and learned his hypothesis has been misinterpreted by three world religions to mean that animals are created by God solely for human use. But he found it interesting from a philosophical-scientific point of view.

That same night, Charles Darwin and Rene Descartes shared their story with us. They told us how they accidentally met at a prestigious Eastern University. The university continues to use Chimpanzees in their students' scientific "research." They found the Chimps are kept in small cages and sleep on cold concrete with no blankets. Many Chimpanzees, our closest relative in the animal kingdom, spend decades in laboratories suffering in various stages of painful, often lethal procedures during what is called "research."

Disturbed, Darwin traveled the rest of the way to Sanctuary wondering why modern science has ignored his final study. It would seem, he thought, his in-depth study of *The Expression of the Emotions in Man and Animals* published in 1872, would be used in tandem with his theories about evolution. Possibly enlighten scientists to realize that the emotional lives of all mammals closely match those of humans. Maybe recognize the complexity of animal personalities and change their attitudes about the true nature of animals. His assumption was that if his research were studied, scientists would treat the other animals as they do themselves.

Descartes was far from being disturbed. He never dreamed his seventeenth century methods of experimenting on dogs without anesthesia would continue to be used three hundred years later in modern-day experimental laboratories. He was proud to see the Cartesian method is the choice of countless experimental laboratories today.

Frustrated by their stories, Guardian pointed out that modern scientists are not slightly interested in testing animals to ascertain whether they have souls. But they are interested in using live animals in the development of consumer products. Every year, millions of animals suffer without anesthesia to determine the "safety" of cosmetics and household products created for human consumption by many companies, including Procter and Gamble and Lever Brothers. Substances in dozens of cosmetics, soaps, cleaning products including oven cleaners are tested without compunction on the eyes, skin and organs of living rabbits, cats, dogs, pigs, rats and even birds.

Teacher added "The same tests are repeated over and over to 'prove' what is already known: certain product's ingredients are toxic to humans or aren't toxic to humans. Scientists know these tests could be replaced with alternative methods of gathering data using computer and imaging technologies. It is not to be. After all, the raising and selling of animals to labs and schools is big business," she said.

Many plates were left uneaten that night. The group returned to their sleeping pods in silence.

The animals were growing agitated by the presence of old antagonists. It was my turn to give them assurance. "I have been asked by the animals to speak for them by using my vocal chords. They want you to know that it is difficult for them to 'open up' because many of you don't believe the other animals are capable of communicating complex thoughts. Skeptic's statement, 'I think; therefore I am' is directed toward humans, and influenced world belief that the other animals are soulless beings."

I turned to face Skeptic as Rene Descartes, and said as gently as I could, "The animals want you to know that many animals do have vocal cords. Every animal species communicates with their own kind, as well as with the other animal species in ways that continue to perplex human understanding." Unmoved, Skeptic turned his back to us and continued writing in his journal. Scientist looked up. He seriously doubted animals could talk at all, but decided for the moment to not enter into a debate.

The moment had come. I stood in the circle waiting for a message to be delivered by the animals. Who would be the first? Minutes passed. I felt as if my head was wrapped in a tight band. I was overcome with dizziness. The trees whirled around me in one direction, and the stars became blinding circles of light spinning above the canopy in the opposite direction. The images in my brain spun out of control. I could see the animals' eyes reflecting encouragement through the nauseating whirl. I held onto their images to anchor my mind. I became incapacitated and fell to the ground to wait for the spinning to stop.

A research Chimpanzee named Billy Jo awkwardly limped into the circle and offered his hand to me. I knew how difficult it was for this shy ape to be among humans. On February 14, 2006, he died. For fourteen years at the "Laboratory for Experimental Medicine and Surgery in Primates," he endured hundreds of surgeries including forty-three liver biopsies, three bone marrow biopsies, and two lymph node biopsies.

Billy Jo's suffering was unnecessary because most experiments using Chimpanzees (or any other animal for that matter) cannot directly benefit human health until humans undertake the same procedures. His thumbs are gone. He chewed them off during the hallucinogenic effect of a tranquilizing, pain-killing drug tested on him. After he died, his life inspired animal Guardians to increase their efforts to free Chimpanzees from further torture in the name of science. It's wonderful seeing him alive here in Sanctuary! He offered his shoulder for me to lean on. He was demonstrating how animals' trust isn't easily broken. The brave fellow squatted on his haunches next to me. How could I falter with Billy Jo beside me?

He tugged on my leg. He is ready. So am I. His thoughts poured into my head, and I found myself speaking in the crackling voice of an elder. I had become Billy Jo. "Thousands of years ago, humans understood at their very core that there was a deep bond between people and the other animals. Their first stories about the sacredness of all life forms can be found on the walls of cliffs and caves. Prehistoric peoples were the first to understand their spiritual connection with the other animals. This knowledge continues to inspire indigenous peoples and is found in the basic tenets of religions around the world."

Not one in the assembly would be able to say they couldn't hear Billy Jo's message. The wind stopped moving the leaves on the trees. The grasses were still. The gurgling sound of the river rapids ceased. Its waters passed silently down to the sea. My heart was beating as fast as Billy Jo's. Using my vocal chords, he spoke forcefully. "Why did the other animals become invisible in your spiritual adventure? Why do you cling to the belief that you are separate and above all other creatures in some sort of hierarchal system?" Billy Jo was in me and I in him. "It is obvious that you select tiny fragments of facts instead of seeing the whole. You are able to access knowledge from across the ages, yet choose to stay ignorant about the true meaning of our co- existence."

I (he) was pleading. "All we ask is that you allow us to live out our natural life cycles without pain. My brothers and sisters of many species are suffering and humiliated because of your beliefs and attitudes toward them." I put my hand on Billy Jo's shoulder. He was shaking. So was I. He hobbled out of the circle and sat directly in front of Skeptic. Descartes craned his neck to see around the big fellow. Billy Jo was making another kind of statement.

My voice grew deeper without any effort on my part. The animals are speaking through me! I became Frog. Croaking, "In this very moment, my species is leaving the Earth forever. We cannot tolerate the changes in the waters and atmosphere brought on by ecological disturbances. Soon Frog will cease to exist."

I barked as Red Fox. "We do our best to stay out of human-driven harm's way. In the wild we spend most of our days avoiding you. We try to figure out where you will show up and mess with our depleting habitat. My mate and kits spend their days in terror of being removed or killed on land where generations of our family have lived" I scratched my rump vigorously before continuing. "Many of us are forced to live alongside humans on what had been our land. We have no choice. Our inherent memory requires us to stay where we have lived for thousands of years."

Choking on the lump in my throat, as Pig I say, "Our sow-mothers are crammed into cages so small that they cannot stand or turn around. They are impregnated and give birth to litters many times under awful conditions before they are butchered." I am sobbing. "Pig breeders and biologists have publicly announced that Pigs have cognitive abilities more sophisticated than three-year-old humans. We are far more advanced in intelligence but you don't want to know how smart we are as long as we are served to you. Who wants to eat an intelligent, sentient being? We have accepted our roles as nourishment for you. All we ask is that you make our dying for your bacon painless!"

As Wolf, I howled mournfully. "Most awful is your murderous betrayal of our trust. We wolves are considered competition by 'hunters' ('sportsmen' they call themselves) who hide in bushes dressed in camouflage holding high tech power rifles with lasers and steel bows designed to never miss a mark. In Alaska, we are victims of the 'sport' of aerial hunting where shooters kill us from the safety of their airplanes. What sort of a thrill do these people get out of killing us?"

Still Wolf, I am growling fiercely. "Hunters pay land-owners to allow them onto their land for target practice. The landowners fence in their land to trap deer, elk, bear, doves and whoever else is unfortunate enough to be born on their land. Lately, animals are trucked onto the land to provide the shooters with more kinds of targets. Some shooters, including their own children, simply walk up and point-blank kill our trusting cousins. The animals don't stand a chance because they haven't learned to fear people.

"They are not killing us because they need our fur or flesh as they did in earlier times. They are killing us because they enjoy the 'sport.' Why do they call us 'game?' Isn't a 'game' a competition between two teams who agree to compete? No animal has ever agreed to play the killing game with these 'sportsmen.'"

Then as Dog, "If we live in your homes as your 'pets,' we offer abject subservience and unconditional love. What do we have to do to get your attention? By believing we are separate from you, you are avoiding your own natural state and living in an unstable, artificial environment. Worse, you need to know that your membership in Nature is expiring!"

Billy Jo is back. "Maybe if you can explain to us why all this is happening to the animal world, we'll share our fate with you willingly. Maybe if you understood what's happening to the human soul, the future of the Earth would be altered."

One by one, the other animals spoke. Hours passed. Finally, my head was empty of their voices. The animals had released me to my own thoughts. It took a moment for me to adjust to the sensation of being "Q" again.

When I was able to speak as myself again, I announced, "Never lose sight of the fact that as Universal Images, you are the highest aspect of every person you embody. As a physical being in this lofty state, you could find yourself in a situation in Sanctuary that is overwhelming, even for you. We are human, after all. However, Sanctuary's environment must remain harmonious or there will be serious consequences."

I hesitated before telling them. "I am not standing before you as my true self. You have the ability to shift into many human forms. I can't. I will remain in a single human form as 'Q' until our sojourn ends. At the moment every one of us agrees with the answer to the animals' question, I will reveal who I am."

The Universal Images looked at each other nervously, and for a moment talked among themselves. As they talked, many shifted into the various images of the people within them. I waited until they turned to face me again. They stared at me for a long time. I couldn't intuit the mood of the group. Their reaction to my announcement made me uneasy, yet I felt safe to continue. I had just delivered a tough message for any human, no matter how complex or wise that being is. For the most part, every Image appeared to trust what I said, and showed a sincere willingness to work together.

Break time. Some retreated to the safety of their sleeping pods to think about what had happened this morning. Some walked into the forest arm in arm. Some stayed in the circle. The animals stayed close by. Their presence was comforting.

WHEN THE CIRCLE ASSEMBLED AGAIN, Cleric as Roman Catholic Priest spoke. "Tiny fragments of knowledge? Billy Jo is right! The Church has always limited the extent of knowledge it wants its members to know about early Christian history. Might confuse them. It always amazes me that my parishioners, who have been carefully guided to uphold their allegiance to the Church, continue to ask questions about the significance of Catholicism in modern times. My job is to make sure that the doctrines are kept a priority in their belief systems. But it's getting harder and harder. People are seeking answers outside of the Church!" Perplexed, Priest scratched under his collar.

Every-Teacher commented, "There are preachers today who threaten damnation in Hell for their followers if they don't follow their interpretations of the Bible. Times haven't changed very much." Then, as if to himself, "Powerless, I lie in my bed at night afraid of the world we find ourselves in. I look forward to my own death. Maybe at that moment I will become what I imagine I really am."

Scientist looked down at his palms as if to find an answer there. "I wonder. Has the human race ever taken what it wants from the Earth's resources without harming another living being in the process? On my darkest days, I think of the human species as a parasite upon the land, seas and skies of our fragile Earth. Our species is destroying it all. Including us!"

Sage said, "There is hope, Scientist. Jainism, a religion established in India, requires its followers to live every day of their life following the path of absolute non-violence toward all living beings. The Jain believe that when their body dies, their soul will return again and again to look out of the eyes of every possible life form. Some Jain, including their children, wear masks so they won't swallow a fly and carry whiskbrooms to sweep the ground so they won't step on an ant. Gandhi modeled his strategy of *ahimsa* from the Jains."

"I admire the Jain for their commitment to the natural world," Healer said. "Modern Jain-owned businesses are primarily in fields of technology where no animal products are used. The Jain religion membership ranks sixth in India and fourteenth in the world. Yet, its adherents enjoy enough prosperity to pay one-half of India's income taxes! Could it be the animals are blessing them for their compassion?"

Guardian asked, "How many followers of the other world religions are taught to practice non-violence toward the other animals?"

"We have the knowledge and wisdom to correct the issues that divide the human race from the rest of the network of life,"

Change Maker said. "Think about it. We slash our rainforests down for cheap wood products sold at mega discount stores. Then we cry over the end of the forests and the mindless killing of animals living in them. We are concerned. We can't be concerned or we'd go insane." Change Maker stared into the fire trying to find the words and then said softly, "How can we make change until we change ourselves into something we have yet to become?"

There was nothing more to say.

Suddenly, a pod of Dolphins leaped out of the Sea spinning so rapidly they formed a giant funnel of water that rose to the surface. Uttering a note that began low-pitched, the Dolphins made a sound that increased in volume until the awful screech cut into every nerve of my body. I held my hands over my ears. Others clutched their bodies until mercifully the pitch rose until it was beyond our capability to hear.

The canines heard the Dolphin cry, ran to the edge of the cliff and jumped into the water. Without hesitating, they leaped into the whirling funnel. The rest of the land and sky animals followed close behind them and flew or swam into the form. Fishes of every color and size were already within the rising maelstrom. The funnel grew higher and higher. We were witnessing a show of unity by the animals so sublime and fearful that some of us wept. Without hesitating, a Guardian of the sea dwellers pulled away from his Universal Image and dove into the expanding whorl. No other human attempted to join the animals. Not yet. Logic prevailed. We knew our abilities. The funnel spun faster and faster until it left the waters and rose into the heavens. In a flash, it disappeared into the cosmic skies.

Oh, no! The animals are in that funnel! In an instant, Sanctuary became empty, without meaning. We stood staring at the sea dumbfounded. We traveled to this place to help the animals. Now they are gone! What should we do? Shoulders drooping, Sage walked away from us and lay face up in the sand. He stretched out his arms and legs as if in supplication. Maybe he was pleading our case with Sanctuary. Whatever he was doing, the animals began to reappear out of the water.

The birds came first. A scraggly wet African Grey Parrot flew out of the water, followed by hundreds of bird species. The air filled with their cries. Cat emerged, shaking his legs. Horse, Moose, Goat and dozens of hoofed ones galloped onto the beach together. The parade of the rest of the animals took hours. Rabbit emerged clutching Tiger's head. Soggy Pig pranced into the circle and rolled on the ground. Dog ran to Skeptic and shook himself, shedding water all over him (to his dismay and our delight). I was beginning to like Skeptic. He has a place in this conference. His reactions counter ours, and that's good for us all.

I hope.

EIGHT
Secret is Out

GUARDIAN AND CHANGE MAKER STOOD at the shore of the sea with their arms around each other. The couple has returned every night. A walk along the shores is not for everybody. Even in moments like these, visitors have learned to stay alert. No telling when an unexpected event might surprise them with another "lesson" from Sanctuary. "Part of the fun of being here," said Guardian.

Their invitation to travel to Sanctuary had come in the knick of time. They are weary and need a break from their intense schedule back on Earth. Change Maker has earned her place in history. She has spent her life seeking justice under the law for women and children. Guardian's time has been divided between protecting animals and working side by side with his partner.

Gorilla stood next to the couple. They welcomed her presence. Dog is sitting not too far away from them. Her eyes are focused on Cat. Cat has come along to see what there is to see. He is a few feet away from everybody, stalking Crab. Crab searches the sand for a bite of food, oblivious to Cat. It's a family thing.

The sea funnel has long gone. It was as if that amazing moment had never happened. Not a memory of movement crosses the Sea's infinite body. The spiraling celestial bodies above are mirrored on the still waters below. There are no ripples on the surface to hint that creatures dwell there. The stars illuminate the deep to reveal life forms are swimming in closer waters. Every few minutes, a Dolphin or Whale leaps out of the still waters into the dark night. The galaxies and nearby stars reflect upon their glistening bodies. The effect is spectacular. More spectacular is the sea mammals' immediate return to the sea quietly, without a ripple.

"No matter how often we come here, the sea takes my breath away," Change Maker said. "The illusion makes me think of the ambivalent conditions found on our world. The sea is tranquil now, but I keep asking, 'for how long?' What mystery will it reveal to us and when?" She whispered, "I can't imagine what my role is in this conference. I know I'm here for a reason. Guess I'll figure it out sooner or later."

He smiled and said, "You already served the gathering when you inspired Q to find the courage to speak." She squeezed his hand. "Right now, I'm glad to be here. We needed a vacation." Guardian chuckled, "Some vacation! Next year, let's go to Hawaii!"

"I always think of the New York skyline at night as the most wondrous sight I'd ever see," Change Maker said, adding, "Was I wrong!"

Guardian stroked Gorilla's head. She signed a "thank you," and "to scratch her back, please." Gorilla has learned hundreds of words using the sign language of the deaf. She is happy to be able to communicate with humans using one of their languages. Her homeland tribe understands each other perfectly using gestures and sounds. She finds it amusing that her human teachers cannot communicate in Gorilla language.

"I wish I had joined the other animals in that awesome funnel. I couldn't react to what was happening fast enough!" He said wistfully.

"Me too," his partner said. "Since then, I've had a hard time sleeping. I wake up wondering what will happen next. It's taken many sleepless nights to get used to the sounds coming from outer space. Can't explain it, but I think I'm hearing the Universe creating itself."

Looking across the sea in awe, Guardian said softly, "So vast and marvelous! Yet, I get the same feeling I do watching a flower open."

Change Maker whispered back, "I didn't know you ever watched a flower open."

He grinned, "I haven't. Saw it happen on a PBS Television documentary once."

She laughed and nudged his waist and leaned down to stroke Dog's head. Cat pushed against her legs looking up for attention too. "What about mee-ow?"

The sweet moment ended with a sound that came from outside of Sanctuary. Was it somewhere in the skies? Or was it somewhere beneath them? A low wail bellowed and moaned across the night air. Change Maker scooped up Cat. Crab dove into the waters. The group hurried back to the circle to find the rest of the people standing close together. Many were in their nightshirts. The sleeping pods would be empty tonight.

A door creaked open from somewhere at the edge of Sanctuary. A door? How could a door exist in this open setting with no walls? It was a door all right. The portal had not been opened – ever! The echoes of its opening reverberated across the cosmos itself. Every scrape, grate, grind, jangle and clank screeched through my bones. No one or no thing could harm us here in Sanctuary. Or could they? I shivered.

Dim light filled Sanctuary. It was the kind of light one sees entering the darkest corners of the mind. "My God!" Cleric said out loud. "The door *is* in my mind!" The group began to get agitated. The clearing filled with an uncomfortable vibration. Some one or some thing had entered Sanctuary uninvited, and was walking toward us.

Who was this strange being? He seemed to be more like a shadow than a figure with substance. Someone recognized him. Fearfully, he uttered his name. "It's Secret!" We all knew who he was, all right. We've heard him in the speeches of world leaders and observed him in the actions of politicians fighting to stay in power. We've seen him in the faces of little schoolgirls whispering in a corner of a playground. I saw him at a circus once. The Elephants, dressed in bright red and gold brocade, walked stiffly around center ring. Ringmaster ceaselessly snapped his whip at their ankles. Ankles made painfully sore by the steel cuffs linked to short chains attached tightly to them immediately after the show. They would remain standing, unable to take a step for hours through the night until the next performance.

Obviously shy, the little guy kept his head bowed as he entered the clearing where we had gathered. Face hidden in a deep hood, he approached us cautiously, his drab robe dragged on the ground. If we didn't know he was there, we wouldn't have noticed him at all. It would be so easy to dismiss his presence.

For the first time since we arrived, we became one mind. And as one mind, we wanted him to go away. Embarrassed by our reaction, we couldn't look at each other. After all, we were invited by the animals to discuss an important question that could affect the very evolution of life on Earth. Who invited this fellow? We've traveled across time and space in peace to get here. He was disturbing it.

Secret spoke. "I've never been outside of you. Ever. I live where no one wants to admit they know me. You keep me buried in the dark shadows of your minds hidden from your friends and families." He appeared to shrink a bit more if that were possible. "Sometimes you don't acknowledge I'm inside you. Sometimes you do. When that happens, I am sent into the abyss of your secret selves where I become lost for days. Often years."

We faced him warily. How could this scrubby being we'd hidden away for so long be walking free outside of our selves? "I don't mind the fire. It's quite lovely. But, please let it get low until I get used to the light?" he said. Walking from person to person, he bowed before each one of us and softly said our names. How could he know our names?

When he approached the animals, the atmosphere changed. "These innocent beings hold no secrets," he said gently. Of course! The animals invited him, even though they knew we would dread his presence. A warm breeze filled the clearing and swept away all our feelings of doubt. Bird song and animal hum resumed. It was going to be a good day after all.

"Wait a minute," Teacher asked. "Why did you come here at this time?" Secret's face opened into the biggest smile a face could make. It was a sweet smile. It reminded me of the smiles of serenity I've seen on sculptured images of Buddha and Quan Yin, and on the faces of cherubim painted by Renaissance artists. Somehow I knew I could trust him even though he made the hair on the back of my head stand up.

In spite of ourselves, we knew if we were to accomplish what we've set out to do, he had to be here. Secret knows the true reasons why people abuse each other and the animals and the environment we share. Because of Secret civilizations crumble, wars wage, belief systems are turned upside down.

The little fellow began to sway, then bobbed up and down in

a curious dance. As he slowly whirled around the fire, he chanted softly. I could hardly hear him. *"You know! You know! You know!"* The sound became a mantra. *"You know, You know,"* he repeated as he passed and pointed to each one of us, dancing faster and faster and faster. The two words became a rhythmic beat that cast a spell on every one of us. The animals hummed in monotone. The chant grew louder, and then softer, then high pitched, then low. *"You know! Know! You know! Know! Youknow, youknow . . . You. You. You. Know Know Know now!"*

With every cadence of the sound, we could feel our innermost selves open up. We knew. We know. We've always known. The sound rose up through the trees and soon every living being in Sanctuary began to sway. In spite of its strange message, it was being delivered sweetly, gently over again and again and again! *"Know now! Know know know . . . Now . . . Now!!"*

We were frightened and thrilled at the same time as the sound filled every cell in our bodies. One by one, we stood up, took someone's hand and joined Secret in his dance. We danced a dance never danced before. Our movements were grace-fuller than any grace that has ever been. Just think! We are the first to "know." We formed a circle linking arms, then put our hands on shoulders and kicked high. We danced for centuries. Or it seemed that way. *"We know! We know!"* We knew. We knew!

When I woke up, the skies above the tree canopy were cast in glow-in-the-dark purples, oranges, yellows and reds. It was another spectacular Sanctuary dawn. My head was on someone's lap. His was on another's shoulder. Her head was mostly on Lion's belly. Lion was sleeping on his back. Small Monkey nestled in his black mane, arms wrapped around the great feline's snout. His long fingers covered his eyes and nose. I wondered how Lion could breathe. He was breathing all right. His snoring was shaking the ground. Perched just above him on a low branch, Parrot mimicked Lion's snores in high-toned nasal pitch. What a quirky concert!

Four were sitting up asleep in an odd square. Scientist, Skeptic and Philosopher's feet were connected toe to toe with Grizzly Bear's enormous paws. Mouse was curled up in Dog's ear. Dog's head was on Skeptic's leg. Dog was drooling. Must be dreaming about a biscuit. I giggled thinking about Skeptic waking up and finding his pant leg soaked by Dog's slimy spittle.

Elves, fairies and odd little gnomes were napping everywhere they could find a crevice. I was surprised to see them here. I'd heard many stories about them as a child but never quite believed they actually existed. They were so tiny! When they noticed I saw them, they instantly left the clearing. Some stretched and flew away. Most popped away like bubbles.

I'd been wondering whom Healer was talking to (besides herself) when she sat under her favorite bush. She had explained to us that unseen energies have taken the forms of imaginary beings found in fairy tales. In this way, some children and a few adults will recognize them and pass the story of their existence on to others. Their purpose is to tend to every living thing – every blade of grass, every flower, every insect, every fish in the sea. (You can imagine how Skeptic reacted to Healer's revelation.)

I never saw the tiny ones again, although I found myself looking for them under every leaf and blade of grass the rest of the days we were in Sanctuary. There is much to learn from the life forms we encounter. Even the ones we cannot imagine.

I looked around the clearing. Healer was on top of Horse who slept standing up. Her head rested on Horse's neck, her arms dangling at her sides. Colt was lying on the ground next to them. Several birds had found shelter in Colt's mane. Two had begun building a nest in his tail. Gorilla had her arms full of Guardian and Change Maker. They were snuggled together so tightly I couldn't see where she and he and she began and ended. Cat's tail peeked out from under the sprawl. Cat wasn't going to leave his new friends' sides.

Sage propped up Cleric, who was kneeling on a makeshift prayer bench holding her prayer beads. Billy Jo knelt beside them. Their eyes were closed, heads bowed. Butterflies and Bees whorled around the three's heads. Behind them, several giant anthills had become part of the landscape. Ants have not been sleeping. I wondered what Cleric would do when she woke up to find her prayer beads moving. Little iridescent Beetles with their tiny legs linked together, were revolving around her hands.

A few others stirred and as we caught each other's eye, we started to laugh at the incongruity of the sight. First a giggle, then a sniggle, then a snigger, then a titter, then a tee hee, then a ha ha, then a haw haw, then a yuk yuk and a hoot and a holler. By now, as each one woke up wrapped in or around some body, yawns became chuckles, then chortles, then thundering tears-in-the eyes, knee-slapping laughter. Dog barked joyfully. Cat mee-hawhawed and Wolf howled. I couldn't breathe! My nose was stuffed with glee. Some of the smaller monkeys, lizards and squirrels were laughing so hard they lost their grip on the branches and tumbled into the fray. Unicorn fell out of her nest whinnying all the way down. The shower of animals floating into our midst made us laugh even more. We rolled on the ground in absolute weak state.

Healer dried her eyes and noticed it first. Where was Secret? He was nowhere to be found. Our laughter slowed down. As we began to breathe again, we reluctantly separated from each other and began to search for him. We looked everywhere. Even in our heads. He was gone. The dark corners in our minds where he'd lived all those years were empty. Now what? Secret was out. We could no longer blame God or our ego or karmic retribution when things don't go our way. We are responsible for our actions.

Without Secret to hide behind anymore, we were exposed, vulnerable. We forgot what we knew. Forgot what he taught us. I longed to go back to our long sleep together. Maybe we'd remember Secret's message. The group walked about in silence. We no longer held hands. The dance had ended. The animals were disappointed by our confusion and returned to the forest in silence. Darkness enveloped Sanctuary.

The seas began to stir.

NINE
What's Happening?

DAYS HAVE PASSED. Maybe Secret's visit was an illusion. When he disappeared our questions about who he was and what he "knew" were left unanswered. Every member of the group was shaken by his visit. People became distant from each other and avoided expressing themselves in the gatherings. I sought refuge in my sleeping pod.

What was Secret telling us? What do we know? Knowing I might never know makes me wonder if I know anything at all. Which I don't. Monkey appeared at my entryway. I said, "Know this, little one. You don't know either. Try sleeping, dreaming, wondering about it. Will the knowing come to you? How will you know?" Monkey scratched his ear, and pronounced "*Know!*" as clear as any human could. He produced a ripe fruit and began to noisily devour it. Fragrant juices dripped onto his chest. His long narrow fingers became sticky with sweet nectar. Just then, the other monkeys and primates began to hoot and howl. Their noise came from many locations in the forest. Monkey tilted his head, dove out of my entry and vanished in the dark. What was that all about? Oh well, I have my own problems right now.

I can't stop asking questions! Why this? Why that? I forget what I want to know, then forget the question and descend into my own Inferno. It's my Inferno. No one else's. Is it arrogance to want to know? Is it arrogance to not want to know? I want to laugh at myself. How can I laugh when I don't get it? I get it all right. Then, I forget what I "got" in the first place.

Lost again. My thoughts tossed from one side of my head to the other. I tried to lie quietly, and watched a newborn Moth explore the ceiling. Only made me more impatient. What did

Secret want us to know? Where will "knowing" get us? Better
not think about it. Thinking is a state of not knowing. (I think . . .)
Some people know. They've known for a long time. They found
the answers but won't share what they know. I'd share. My mind
spun round and round, down and down. I sank into my pillow
and finally drifted off to sleep.

CR

It's ALMOST DAWN. My sleeping pod is filled with a strange blue
mist. Thick moisture covers everything. I should have closed my
leaf shades last night. Had the moisture come in from the seas?
Maybe Sanctuary was disturbed by our inability to understand
Secret's revelation. I lowered my pod to the ground. The fog was
getting heavier. I couldn't see past my fingertips. As I crawled
out, my hands sunk into oozy mud! Mud?

A huge dark form entered the clearing. It's Elephant! She
passed me without looking up and disappeared in the damp
grasses. "Hey!" I whisper-shouted (didn't want to wake anyone
up). She turned toward me for a moment but kept walking away.
Where was she going? Her baby, always close by, was nowhere
to be seen. His favorite berry patch probably slowed him down.
I thought I noticed a trickle of blood on her ear. Blood? Couldn't
be! She must have scraped herself on a branch she didn't see in
the dark.

The morning light is drying the dank. We need the warmth
of the light. Especially this morning. As I approached the circle,
many were already seated. Seems no one slept very well last
night. Billy Jo and Dog were waiting patiently for the group to
arrive. Cat crawled into my lap. I gratefully buried my nose in his
fur. Bear and Deer entered together. Elephant and her baby were
next. I was relieved to note the giant had bathed that trickle of
blood off her ear.

Parrot landed on a branch of a small tree. I think I heard Tree
say, "Be careful, bird! You might crack the branch. Now look at
what you've done! One of my leaves has fallen!" Parrot picked
the leaf up and brought it to Tree. Leaf promptly joined with the
branch again. The bird said to Tree, "See? All better again. You
are magnificent, Tree." Tree stretched and apologized for her
reaction. "I hope you understand. I'm a nervous wreck. Since *they*

arrived in Sanctuary, nothing is the same. I miss the peaceful life we had before the humans came."

Skeptic leered at Tree. "Even the plants are getting too smart for their own good!" he mumbled. A perfect moment to let off steam! Good old Skeptic! He always can get us to laugh! Imagine a tiff with a Tree! His bewilderment at our reaction set off another round of chuckles.

We were ready to work again. Teacher spoke first. "I think Secret was trying to direct us to some Universal truth we need to know if we are to answer the question." Then hesitating, he said, "But knowing the truth can be dangerous." Skeptic stopped writing in his journal to nod his head in agreement. Maybe Skeptic has decided to join the discussion.

Teacher absently picked up a small white mouse and placed him onto his shoulder. "I'm afraid of myself. Afraid for myself. I haven't the courage to admit the truth that I am a fraud in my classroom. My job is to open the doors in my students' minds by showing them all sides of issues and guiding them to make their own decisions. Lately my lectures are turning into sermons. I find myself trying to change the world by convincing my students to adopt my ideas." He gently lifted the wee one from his shoulder and placed him in his shirt pocket. The little guy happily peeked out from the pocket opening feeling safe in his new shelter. Teacher added, "Come to think of it, I keep my innermost beliefs deep inside me where no one (not even my partner) can enter. Somehow, Secret has disturbed me, but not changed me."

Change Maker said tentatively, "The more I think about our task, the more impossible it seems." Philosopher looked at Change Maker as if for the first time. "Change Maker, I am disappointed that you find our task impossible. You have been in the global driver's seat many times and successfully inspired large populations to accept your views. For better or worse, you have rewritten world history."

"For better or worse?" She was about to challenge the comment, when Communicator said, "I think our reality is shaped by our own experiences. My reality is different than yours. Hundreds of animals have shared their thoughts with me in detail. I am always amazed when they report their mistreatment at the hands of humans without resentment. I sense they have compassion for their abusers much as a parent has for an unruly child. It's a miracle that the animals speak to us at all."

The animals moved in to be closer to Communicator. Birds appeared with flowers and arranged them in a makeshift crown on her head. Some dropped petals around her feet. The smaller animals raced to find a place in her lap. So many jumped on her at the same time, she disappeared in a mass of life that nestled on and in her garment. The sight was funny, touching, and a bit uncomfortable to witness. Laughing, she said, "Trouble is, few humans accept the fact that the animals are 'speaking' to us. Fewer yet are willing to listen to them."

Philosopher stood. His form was becoming translucent. I could see the men and women contained within him. They were moving in and out of his body. I looked around. The other universal forms were in the same stages of transformation. He suggested we move quickly to resolve the subject at hand. Our time in Sanctuary was running out.

Cleric emerged from Philosopher's form. This was something new. Universal beings emerging from other Universal beings! I looked into the eyes of the people and the other animals to see if they found this new change confusing. They didn't. I did. Cleric had become the form of a renowned televangelist shown on a paid-for cable television channel. The minister walked over to the center of the clearing and dramatically cleared his throat. "There is only one thing that interests people. They are concerned about their own souls and what happens to them after they die. I am personally told by Gawd to remind you that you have dominion over the other animals and all the Earth!"

Clearly upset, Communicator shouted at Cleric, "I am so sick of you and your religions!" I think I saw a small dark cloud forming in the skies. "In every society where religions dominate the laws and politics of the land, the other animals have been denied their souls. How can we get anywhere in these meetings if the animals have already lost the game?"

"Wait a minute, Communicator!" Scientist was vibrating. "Has anyone ever seen a 'soul?' There is no measurable proof that any sort of spirit or soul exists. And, if there is such a thing, there is no proof 'it' continues to exist after the body dies. Until the spirit, soul, life force (whatever you, Cleric . . . Philosopher . . .

Sage . . . and whoever else getting in on the act call it) can be seen and measured you'll never convince me that your ethereal, metaphysical mumbo jumbo is valid. Never will!" Shaken, Communicator started to fade in and out. The animals moved closer as if to prevent her from leaving.

Canada Goose waddled into the midst of the circle. His head hung down almost to the ground. I wasn't the only one who thought his neck was broken. It wasn't. His depression was that deep. He spoke, "Please don't fight! We will never settle the question if you fight. It's really rough out there. My species is constantly in a state of confusion. We never know whether we are 'endangered' and protected by law, or declared 'sport' animals to be 'culled' by hunters. We utilize the Earth's magnetic fields to guide us during our migration. We know no other routes. It's impossible to avoid the human zones. Some towns place border collies, swans and electronic fences to prevent us from taking a rest stop in their parks and water havens. Can you imagine? The very waterways where we've taken refuge for centuries are closed to us because we are 'bothersome.'

"We can't land in a tree like Sparrow or nest in rocky cliffs like Eagle. Sometimes we are delayed from our travels for days searching the landscape for friendly waters. Many of us, weakened by hunger and exhaustion, drop to the ground and feed on whatever grasses and seeds we can find. Some can't regain their strength and must wander where they landed for the rest of their days. The flock must go on."

The forest had grown quiet. The prey animals crouched in the grasses watching with great interest. "Don't get me wrong," he continued. "Not all humans are our enemies. I especially like to land in a pond where children are playing. I enjoy the chase when they run up to us thinking they're scaring the flock. Their delightful screams always make us laugh as we fly away.

"We were once a proud, abundant race. There were so many of us hundreds of years ago that when our flocks flew across the Nebraska skies you'd think night had overcome day. Sure, we'd lose a fair number to people and the other animals needing food. We have always understood that nourishing others is an aspect of our life cycle. But times have changed.

"At the Canadian border when the hunting season begins,

hundreds of cars, pickups, hummers, RV's, even limousines set up camp. The hunting season coincides with our migration patterns. As we pass over the border into the United States lands, from our great height we hear the noise of the shooting. We do our best to fly over the range of the high-powered rifles, machine guns and shotguns (whatever the shooters can get their hands on). We hear them shouting, 'Bet I can knock off more than you can! Aim for the leader bird!'"

Goose's neck curved up in anger. Hissing, "The leader bird is always one of our strongest females. Don't they know that? Would it make any difference to them if they knew? Last season, my tribe was crossing a lake when my mate was shot down. She was the strongest in our flock and usually led us across the sky. I stayed with her as long as I could. She whispered to me to go on, that she'll be fine, and hoped she would be a nourishing dish for the hunter's family." Goose began to shake as he recalled the event. "Always the wise one, she was. We geese mate for life, you know.

"So many of us are killed at the same time that our bodies are not picked up. At night, we huddle in a refuge pond or lake to discuss our future. Look, we know we are tasty to eat and have been widely praised for our flesh's flavor. That's not my complaint. It's the waste. The awful waste of killing simply to kill. All we are asking for is some acknowledgement that we have a rightful place in the natural world."

Wolf walked up to the great bird and dropped a mouthful of seed grasses at his feet. She licked the top of his head, and thanked him for bringing sustenance to her cubs. Goose looked up amazed at Wolf's gesture. He stretched his wings. There was a hum of awe around the circle when we saw the breadth of their span. He looked at the many loving faces smiling at him, raised his long neck straight, and took a spot next to Fox.

Cleric had been busy shifting from persona to persona. This time he stepped forward in red robes befitting a high level office in the Roman Catholic Church. He had become a heavy bull of a man who moved slowly and deliberately as he walked into the circle. It was Thomas Aquinas himself! He pronounced magnanimously, "According to Divine ordinance, the life of animals and plants is preserved not for themselves but for man.

There is no sin in using a thing for the purpose for which it is!"

Wolf's eyes were menacing, her teeth bared, "Using a *Thing* for the purpose for which it is? Is that how you heard Goose's story? Are you saying Goose is a *Thing*?" Wolf's legs were spread apart as if she was about to spring. "Then you, sir, are a dumb ox! You people insult each other by calling each other 'animals,' 'pigs,' 'asses,' 'chickens.' Why can't you respect us?

"Sometimes, animal courage is tested beyond any situation a human could tolerate. Consider the male Emperor Penguins who stand for nine weeks in the freezing violence of the dark Antarctic winter to keep one egg warm. One egg! Their mates battle the same storms traversing hundreds of miles to the sea to find food, then endure the same awful conditions to return to care for their chicks and to breed again. All animals endure the worst of conditions to preserve our young and our species. Can't you see our resemblance to you?" Wolf snarled, "Cleric, where do you get these words? From God? I think they come from a fat man like you who eats through his days! If this is 'animal,' I am proud to be animal standing before you."

I thought, after living eighteen years with my beloved Cat Bhapu, I learned just how complex animal personalities are. He died in my arms a year ago, so you can imagine my delight seeing him here in Sanctuary. We had been inseparable. He'd travel on the plane (carrier in my lap until the flight attendant asked me to put him under the seat), ride in the car (on my shoulder until I was arrested because he was "a distraction"), was a welcome guest in my friends' homes (we always brought his litter box), and had his own sitter when I was called away on business. He liked being "dressed" in a harness and leash. "Because this way we are connected," he once told an animal Communicator.

We played a game when he was feeling especially affectionate (usually at night). I'd settle in on my bed to read when he would silently appear and curl up next to me and close his eyes. I'd take his paw and hold it in my hand. He would gently squeeze my fingers. One day, I squeezed back. Eyes still closed, he squeezed my fingers again. Then it started. He'd squeeze two times. I'd respond with two. My turn. One, two, three. Then he would deliver one, two, three squeezes. I knew he was telling me he understood me.

One warm summer night Bhapu changed my worldview forever. I awoke to see him sitting at the window of our bedroom. His white fur was glowing in the moonlight. I knew he was longing to go outside and find that black cat that often meandered into our alley to taunt him. I looked at him lovingly. I never got weary of his graceful beauty. As I watched him, I was astonished to see a transparent "twin" matching the shape of his body moving in slow motion frame-by-frame until his "twin" leaped out of the window. Bhapu remained in the room. He sat looking out the window as if nothing had happened. I rubbed my eyes to make sure I was awake. I was. He turned and looked at me. I said out loud, "Who are you?" He paused, then easily jumped onto the bed and sat on my chest.

He began another game we often played, "*Who can outstare who?*" I repeated, "Who are you?" As we stared into each other's eyes, his began to shine brightly as if a candle were being held in back of them. My mind started to race. This couldn't be happening! How wonderful that it is happening! No wonder the Egyptians believed that Cat's eyes reflect the sun; and therefore reflect the sun god; and therefore, are Divine, and should be worshipped. My mind raced to accept what I was seeing. Other thoughts poured in to dispute what was happening. As we continued to stare into each other's eyes, I gave in first. I looked away for a brief second to get my bearings and calm my excitement. When I returned my gaze, his eye-light faded, then shut down. Just his silhouette remained. With that, he leaped off the bed and into the dark of the hallway. He'd answered my question. He would never again repeat his message in such a direct way. You can imagine my disappointment in myself for doubting what I saw.

THAT ONE SUMMER NIGHT abruptly changed my understanding of the nature of existence and shifted the direction of my spiritual journey. From then on, every moment I spent with my Cat was sacred to me. My four-legged friend became my most significant spiritual teacher. Every day he reminded me that there was much to learn from him. I wish every human being on Earth would experience what I experienced. Maybe then all animals would be valued as individual personalities with complex lives unique to each one. Certainly, be valued as sentient beings. Maybe this is the message Bhapu wanted me to deliver. Maybe.

Elephant entered the circle and faced Cleric who was still in the image of Thomas Aquinas. "You believe that the other animals were given to you by the 'Creator.' We willingly went along with your myths thinking you would finally notice our connection to you."

She looked around the circle before saying, "I implore all of you to step in on our behalf wherever you see animals suffering. Stop the profiteering! You have seen Elephants dancing in your circuses in front of crowds we fear, and coping in zoo enclosures too small for us. 'Trophy hunting' on private and government land in South Africa is lucrative for the safari planners and the government. Well-equipped, smartly dressed hunters wanting a souvenir horn, skin or head easily kill rhinos, lions, and many other endangered species. The legs of my family are turned into coffee tables."

Elephant paused. "It's not the work, dear ones. We would work in partnership with you willingly if you threw away the whip and treated us fairly." Suddenly, Elephant swung around. Where was her baby? We heard a soft rumbling sound. "Let's go!" her weeks' old son whimpered. He was just out of her line of vision. Talk about blind spots! The mother responded with a firm reverberating snort. "I'm talking!" she trumpeted. Baby hid further behind his mother. "But I'm bored! I wanna play!"

Cow stepped forward and described the great taming wars when her ancestors, the Aurochs, fought for their freedom. "Pain wins. It always does." She said in resignation, "Right now, millions of my sisters are kept in stalls, their heads locked all day in braces preventing them from moving to even scratch their behinds when those awful flies bite."

Cow's big brown eyes filled with tears. "After four or five years, when we are no longer able to produce milk, we are turned into ground beef. Most hamburgers come from dairy cows, you know. We understand our meat is delicious, but aren't there more humane ways to get your food from us?"

Elephant and Cow stood together in the circle. Elephant wrapped her trunk around Cow's neck. Her baby leaned against Cow's legs. Then the animals surprised us. Heads lowered, several entered the circle and humbly bowed to each person. "You are the masters of survival of the fittest," said Gorilla. "We defer to you not only because you have the means to control us, but because we know we belong together. We dream of living with you in harmony. It can be done. You would not be disappointed. I meditate all day hoping for such a world."

"Oh for crying out loud!" Skeptic leaped to his feet. A chilly wind crossed the clearing. The leaves in the trees and the grasses rustled frantically. "We humans <u>are</u> superior to the other animals. My students and I nailed Dogs to boards and experimented on them without using anesthesia. The Dogs' shrieks sounded like the turning of rusty wheels of a machine. Machines have no souls, therefore the shrieks could not possibly have been the cries of living souls!

"I stand by my premise! If you animals were equal to humans in the eyes of God, God would have given you the ability to speak in human tongue. For the life of me, I don't understand how you are speaking to us here in Sanctuary. It's demonic! I think this debate is demonic! God gave you to humankind to be our food, clothing, and whatever else we want and need. Period!"

Still shouting, "Look at Raven over there. He's been sitting on that branch for hours staring at us. Shoo! Shoo! Go away, you ugly thing! I don't understand why God created your species!" Raven looked down unemotionally as Skeptic ranted, "You, Raven, are useless to humans. You don't even taste good. I am in charge here. Not you! You are useless to humans. You can't be tamed easily, won't work for me and certainly are not of interest to me scientifically. You're sneaky and devious. I swear you are of the devil. If anything, you are the antithesis of mankind. Be gone, foolish bird!"

Wait a minute! I know this particular bird. We met last year behind a fast food diner. I was cutting through an alleyway trying to avoid the traffic and got stuck behind a garbage truck anyway. Raven was lunching on a half-eaten sandwich he'd pulled out of a torn paper bag. He was perfectly at ease poking around the smelly garbage bin. His beak was full of crumbs. I noticed that he had one eye and was missing a toe on his right foot. As I admired his size and the sheen on his ebony body, he turned and looked at me. I slowed my car down and lowered my car window. His neck feathers rose in warning and he stretched his wings. I called out,

"Don't be afraid of me!"

He laughed (at least it sounded like a laugh). "You are so arrogant!" he said in a low guttural tone. "You have shot me, poisoned me, run me over, and built shopping malls on my natural habitat. This land you drive that big gas-guzzler on has been Raven territory for eons. Afraid? Hardly! Look at me scrounging in your disgusting garbage! More often I am forced to eat the poor souls you crush on your highways. Carrion, you call it. You've turned our fields into concrete and killed off the smaller animals we normally consume. Right now I am trying to grab a bite before that garbage truck comes along!"

I got out of my car and walked toward him. He didn't fly away but stayed for the debate. "You kill other animals!" I said. "You're a killer, too. We all kill. The planet Earth is an eat or be eaten world."

The largest of black birds shouted, "You humans are the height of naivety! You are the supreme destroyers and you know it," he retorted. "There was a time when my cousins Crow, Mynah, Black Bird and I spent our days enjoying the abundance of our beautiful world. Now, all we have is our dignity."

I felt like a school kid being chastised by my teacher. I thought I was being friendly, but he had interpreted my action to be condescending. I suppose in my deepest secret self I knew I was.

Raven continued to peck at the garbage seeking something edible. "Although, I must say this Cod is delicious. Wanna bite?"

A few days ago, Cockatoo told me about a great Raven who had accepted a leadership role among the other animals in Sanctuary. When the animals early on expressed doubt about organizing this conclave with humans in attendance, he motivated them to move forward. Now, this marvelous Raven has revealed himself to the humans! I was thrilled to be in his presence again.

He cleaned a bit of rock from his three-toed foot, then rose and hovered over Skeptic for long terrible seconds. I began to worry. What was Raven going to do? He easily cut through the tree branches and soared above us hundreds of feet performing a set of maneuvers in the sky that no human or human-made flying machine could ever imitate. Then whirling just above Skeptic's head, he shot straight up until we could no longer see him. We watched the heavens wondering where he'd appear next.

Raven suddenly landed on the rock that Skeptic was using to hold his teacup. Not a drop was spilled. The magnificent bird said, "Dear one, when you can do what I have just done, we will talk about 'superiority.' A word that is merely a relative term."

He winked at me. He remembered our encounter! He had one eye, but I knew it was a wink. Best of all, he hopped onto the boulder I was sitting on. I saw the twinkle of his soul in his eye and managed to suppress a wink back. He looked around the circle and announced, "Your task can no longer be centered on your personal interests and needs. Never lose sight of the animals' question!"

His voice rang throughout the forest, *"What happened to the animal-human spiritual connection?* If you doubt we have a connection, simply look into the eyes of the animals you control. The eyes of the animals in laboratories tell you, 'Please! Not that needle again, please!' Shock at man's betrayal is in the eyes of food animals as the doors into the killing rooms swing open."

Raven rose into the air and hovered above us ominously until he dropped to a branch just above Humanity. Looking down at her, he spoke contemptuously, "The same arrogant human attitude prevails all over the world. No animal besides the human animal would use stone traps to catch and crush millions of songbirds a year." His voice was choking. "Think about it! Millions of innocent birds are put on the menus of up-scale restaurants in France, Italy and Greece where food is not scarce for their patrons! What pleasure can people get from chewing on the small bodies of such gifted, gentle beings? Even I who will eat anything was repulsed when I mistakenly ate the bones of a Thrush tossed in a garbage bin in an alley behind a respectable restaurant in Paris. What a waste!"

Black Bear entered the circle cautiously. He obviously feared us. "Hundreds of my cousins unlucky to be living in China and Vietnam are exploited for use in 'traditional medicine' markets," Bear sobbed.

Guardian walked over to Bear and stroked his back. "Yes, it's true," Guardian said. "The Bears are imprisoned in cages little bigger than themselves. This prevents the poor creatures from moving while their bile is extracted from a tube inserted through their abdomen and into their gall bladder. The process is called 'milking.' Guardians who have witnessed the cruelty first-hand report that the Bears' pain is so excruciating that they moan, bang their heads against their cages, and chew on their own paws. When they stop producing bile (after a few years of this torture), they are killed for their meat, fur, paws, and gall bladders. Bear paws are considered a delicacy in Asia," he said.

"Oh God!" Cleric stood up and cried, "I can't bear to hear another story!" He rocked in his seat, holding his ears.

Guardian continued, "Sorry, Cleric, for your discomfort, but it is important for all of us to understand the scope of the situation we are facing. The plight of the Bears is one of thousands of examples of how we, the 'masters' of the Earth, use animals as commodities. Across Asia, countless endangered species are killed, dried, and consumed in concoctions that the people believe will cure them from everything from fertility to baldness to the common cold. The practices have gone on for thousands of years. Surely, the increasing populations of educated people in these countries know by now that dried animal parts cannot heal anything."

Overwhelmed with grief, Bear wandered out of the circle to find refuge in the forest. I wanted to go with him.

Guardian wasn't through. "In the United States we may not 'milk' Bear bile, but gunners are given legal licenses from the states to 'cull' their population. In North America, Bear, Wolf and Mountain Lion have kept the Elk and Deer populations balanced for thousands of years."

I agreed with Guardian, and told the group my story about my first close encounter with free Bears last September, vacationing in the mountain town of Aspen, Colorado. "I'd never seen Bears outside of zoo cages," I said. "The scene was surreal. It was hazy and hot. My friend and I were about to eat an early supper somewhere cool when we spotted a group of people gathered on a street corner. They were silently staring at a small tree shaking violently. Ironically, the tree was growing in a sidewalk hole just outside a fur salon. A small Black Bear was sitting on a high branch hungrily feeding on crab apples. Her two scrawny cubs waited below to grab what she tossed to them. The cubs wrestled over the bits of fruit scattered on the ground. They were paying no attention to the people. I must say, the crowd's sympathy was with the Bears, although the children's parents held onto their hands tightly."

With that, Black Bear returned to the circle and sat down next to me. The group applauded his brave comeback. Someone brought a bowl of fruit to him, and stroked his head. I continued, "The Bears must have been desperately hungry to leave the 'safety' of the wild to find food in an urban area. They had avoided detection and the dangers of busy traffic to find this particular fruit-bearing tree.

"The police cordoned off the tree and tried to get the bears to leave peacefully. Would you leave with hundreds of people surrounding you? At no time did the mother Bear appear to be dangerous to the humans. Hungry? Yes. Dangerous? No. Ultimately, the mother and her cubs were drugged and transported a hundred miles away from their natural habitat. The idea was they would be able to find living space in the territory of a strange Bear clan. Odds were not in their favor."

As the stories about the other animals' struggles to survive unfolded, Humanity couldn't contain herself any longer. Her body began to grow to great height. She rose up until she was about fifteen feet high and appeared to be half as wide! Surprisingly, the animals didn't run away from her. I wanted to get away but was frozen in my seat.

The giantess uncrossed her legs and started to tap her feet furiously. The trees shook, and the smaller animals bounced. Clearly agitated, she spoke for the first time. We were confused by the sound and had to listen carefully. Her "voice" was a chorus of millions of people speaking in unison in complex chord. It seemed we were hearing the sound of every man and woman on Earth speaking at the same time. The sound was awesome, eerie, overpowering . . . awful! Humanity had become the many!

The voices spoke in a rhythmic, even-pitched cadence.
I imagined a drum beating out the words:

> *"Bears?*
> *Bears live far away from my thoughts.*
> *Out of sight, out of mind,*

I always say.
I'm sorry for the bears, but
every nation on Earth has the right
to do what it pleases with its resources
And that's that!!"

The chorus "voice" dropped to low pitch and wailed,

"Get me out of here!
I want to go home!
Somebody – anybody! –
show me the way back home?"
Then, screaming –
"I mean it! Let me go home!
This meeting does not serve me.
Humanity must survive!
It is the law of the Universe!!"

The chorus "voice" withdrew. Humanity sat down, folded her hands, and lowered her head. We sat dumbfounded. We had just listened to the "voices" of Humanity describing a reality on Earth that we hadn't faced yet. Maybe the other animals don't have a chance to be included in humans' spiritual lives, and that is their fate. Skeptic had been trying to tell us all along. His quirky reactions toward what was happening around him never failed to break us up in laughter. We knew that Skeptic wasn't trying to be funny, but we laughed anyway. We mocked him because we thought our views were much wiser than his.

Humanity stood up. She had more to say. The voices within her surprised us with a sorrowful lamentation,

"It's my fault!
I've been taught that God and Heaven are for humans –
not animals.
I believed my teachers.
I believed, I believe,
I believe!
I'm sorry!"

She fell to her knees. The voices became a deep-low, monotone mantra, repeating over and over again.

"So sorry . . .
So sorry . . .
What can we do?"

Then she returned to her "normal" size, which relieved us all. Cleric was about to comment on Humanity's rant by delivering one of his own, when Keeper stood up, stretched, and grasped the bars of his cage. Humanity's words were forgotten when the bars crumbled and crashed to the ground. They were straw! Keeper could have escaped his cage easily! The hoofed animals galloped to where he stood and enjoyed a feast of what had been his prison. He shouted, "It's over! I'm free!" He happily danced in the mess, tossing the straw up in the air. Dozens of birds joined the play by catching broken bits and dropping them back on our heads. Laughing and still covered with straw, the group finally settled in. Keeper had taken center stage.

Pacing back and forth and talking at the same time, Keeper said, "Thank you, Humanity! Your anguish has moved me to admit to myself and all assembled here the secret I'd kept secret from my colleagues, the animals in my care, and the public who paid to see them. Zoos are simply businesses, I'm sad to say. You would think I would have stopped the exploitation. I was the only zoologist placed on the staff. The zoo's board of directors hired me as some sort of token, I'm sure. I took the job because I have six kids.

"Most people don't realize that zoos often stay open long after dark. Parades, light shows and concerts add to the price of admission. All that activity agitates the animals. Many zoos in the United States spend the admission money they charge their visitors to build bigger souvenir shops or fast food stands and fun rides. The animals need a break from the crowds and noise." He hesitated before adding, "Please remember, there are a few zoos in the world who do honor and care for the animals in their charge without resorting to carnival-like programs. The money they collect is actually used to improve the animals' health and quarters. But these zoos are rare."

Healer raised her hand to ask a question but Keeper would not be interrupted.

"Early on in my prison, I figured out who my captors were. Not once did I credit them to be intelligent beings conscious of themselves and others. My ordeal in Zone might have ended sooner if I'd opened my mind about them from the beginning. I became my own jailer and my own prisoner. At the very moment I faced what I'd hidden for so long, I was free to go!" He shook his head in remorse.

I didn't expect what happened next. Keeper's face composed. His eyes became emotionless, indifferent. It was as if his discovery was simply a passing thought expressed by any Scientist in the middle of describing his research. Keeper never again appeared as a separate personality. He would remain one among the many occupying the Universal Image of Scientist for the rest of the time we were in Sanctuary.

Scientist spoke, "I think Secret is unnamable. How can we name something we can't prove existed in the first place? How can we look for an answer to a secret we can't even identify? The secret will have to remain as much of an enigma as the human soul is."

Philosopher walked over to the Scientist shaking a fist. "You, Scientist, are stuck in your brain! Why you are here in Sanctuary is a mystery to me. Secret is describable! Once we understand the meaning of his message, we will be exalted!"

Cleric was afraid. "Secret can never be revealed to the world! Look at what happened to Adam and Eve! They were banished from Eden when they questioned the unknown. Frankly, I can't get involved. Best to keep my mouth shut. Avoid trouble."

Skeptic's face contorted with anger. "Good God! Are you people mad? You speak of Secret as if he exists! Secret was a hallucination, a vapor, a figment of our imaginations! We experienced a group dream, that's all. Let it go, and let's be on with it!" The animals became restless again. Some returned to the quiet of the forest.

"People sure like to talk," Bear said.

Sage said, "I think it's all a matter of belief. I believe one way. You another. Look at you, Scientist. After a bit of squabbling with the religionists and each other, you continue to dedicate your time and resources to prove Evolution is true. Admit it! Evolution started out as an idea based on a belief and remains an idea based on a belief, nothing more."

Scientist's eyes betrayed his surprise. "You are right, Sage. If I am to be true to myself, your logic is impeccable. However, scientific theories are tested using stringent research methodologies and are not dependent on blind faith."

Sage was about to respond when Teacher interjected, "I wonder. What would life on Earth be like if the other animal species intellectually analyzed every step they took, broke it down into endless parts, and disagreed over the details? Thank goodness the other animals' minds are uncluttered!"

Secret had tossed a time bomb in our laps. How can we know the unknowable? Even these great Universal Images out of history and living in the present cannot come to an agreement. As representatives of every kind of thinking and every thought and every belief ever believed about the animal-human connection, they are time bombs themselves.

Lowering her head to my ear, Giraffe sneered, "The humans stumble in the dark separate and divided by their never-ending ideas. We know what the Secret is. We could help them, but they don't think we are capable!"

Filled with my own doubts, all I could do was reach up and stroke her cheek.

Several weeks passed. Or was it minutes? Trying to establish "time" has been a meaningless exercise in this marvelous place where there is no single sun casting shadows at regular hours. I suppose the only time we think about time is when we sense it is rest-time or time to eat. No one noticed Sanctuary's waters expanding and deepening as we debated.

One morning, we found ourselves looking out over a vast ocean. An island had risen out of its midst and we were on it! Some sensed that the restless waters were a singular living entity. Philosopher suggested the Sea might be speaking to us using its waves as its vocal cords. Healer agreed. "Listen to the waves!" she said. "As they move in and out from the shore, the waves seem to be saying, 'Know the truth. Know the truth. Know the truth." Sanctuary is here. But where is here? What is out there?

One morning, Skeptic entered the clearing more agitated than usual. "I couldn't sleep a wink last night thinking about how much longer I can tolerate this crazy place," he complained.

"Science is my master and Philosophy my art! If I return to my times and acknowledge what has happened here, my reputation and my place in history will be gone. What will happen to my conclusions about the presence of animal soul? As far as I am concerned, the other animals are soulless mechanicals, nothing more! This nonsense doesn't even belong in Hell! All of you go to Hell!" He was so angry, he stuttered, "How can mankind progress when people like you twist Science and Religion into fantasy?"

Scientist morphed into the persona of Charles Darwin. Darwin was weary of this pompous man who refuses to cooperate with our work and disputes everyone around him when he doesn't get his way. The two men from two centuries walked toward each other until they were face-to-face, fists up in boxing position. The moment they touched noses, their bodies instantly transformed into two big Mountain Sheep. They were transported onto a cliff that appeared at the edge of the clearing. Heads down, they crashed together, horns butting horns. Their battle was ferocious. When they came close to killing each other, mercifully they were restored to their human forms.

The antagonists' climb down from their lofty site was treacherous, and they tripped and stumbled most of the way. They had to hold onto each other to make the descent. The group stifled their laughter at their clumsy antics. Change Maker and Guardian waited for them on the ground and offered their hands for support. The two men returned to the clearing looking, well, sheepish. Very sheepish, indeed. Healer waved and pointed to seats for one to her right and the other to her left. They glared at each other, rubbing their foreheads. They had matched wits and accomplished nothing. Healer put her hands on both of their shoulders. For a moment, I thought I saw the three engulfed in light.

Clearly upset, Cleric said, "I'm afraid. If we take what we have learned here in Sanctuary back to people in our times, we'll be stoned to death. That happened to me in other lifetimes, and believe me, it's a painful way to go. The human race is not ready for change. Mark my words! Once Secret is revealed and understood by people worldwide, our cultures . . . civilizations . . . histories . . . will be changed forever. We'll go back to the Ice Age. We'll be like the godless Neanderthals again. Every step we've made will have to be repeated. Science will be challenged and ousted (which is all right with me). As for Religions . . ." His face reflected real terror. "What if religions disappear? Where will God go? What will God do? We need God to take care of us. Think about it!"

Scientist said, "Cleric, we are not sure whether the Neanderthals believed in gods or not." After pausing for a long moment he said, "Maybe you are right. We'd better proceed more carefully." The animals watched us in silence. They had begun to doubt whether we were capable of thinking at all.

Cleric clutched the symbol of his religion hanging around his neck. "Look, our traditions are clear. God created humans to lord over the other animals by giving us dominion over the Earth and the ability to make choices." Looking over his shoulder as if to check to see if his God was watching, he whispered, "I hate to admit it, but when Secret opened the door to my mind, he revealed another worldview to me. Until he did, everything I said, did, and believed separated me from other people and the rest of the animals." Cleric touched his forehead, then his lips, then his heart, and clutched his body as if in pain. Sobbing, he shouted into the skies, "Dear God, forgive me for my blasphemy!"

Time is passing quickly.
No one seems to be noticing the rising chill.

TEN
Breakdown

THE GROUP HAS ASSEMBLED IN THE CLEARING. Teacher is speaking. "I'm reminded of a young man who lives in a rural area in Brazil. Scientists and parapsychologists are studying his amazing connection with animals. He can put his hand in a poisonous snake's hole, and the snake becomes putty in his hands. Fish go into a trance as he picks them up out of the water. When a circus came to his town, he sneaked into the Lion cage and sat safely among the great felines. People were astounded that he could do this without getting mauled. He doesn't have the analytical ability to discuss how he does it. All he says is it's a gift from God. I think it is some sort of expanded consciousness. There's something that vibrates from his body's energy that the animals trust. I have a feeling that there are others who have the same ability . . . "

She is interrupted mid-sentence. It sounded as if a stampede of a thousand horses was approaching! Where were they coming from? I held my ears. The hoof beats emanated from a flaming form descending from the skies – fast! Fireworks flashed across the horizon. The forest revealed thousands of eyes. As suddenly as the light and sound show began, the pure black space of the cosmos returned.

Something huge and remarkably light floated down. An enormous Bull landed in the clearing so softly that not even a leaf stirred. He must have been at least nine feet tall at his shoulders! His horns, twenty feet across from one tip to the other, were solid gold. The gold glistened in that pure yellow light that only gold can do. Sitting astride the magnificent being was a woman dressed in denim and riding boots. She held a newborn pig under one arm, and what appeared to be a featherless, tiny bird under the other. "Sorry I'm late!" she laughed. "What a landing!" said one. "I thought we were goners," said another.

Easily dismounting without disturbing her load, a new image of Scientist, the renowned Scientist, Temple Grandin joined us. The baby started to squirm in her arms, and squealed, "Let me down! I want to play!" She released the little piglet who immediately raced around the circle from person to person nuzzling every hand offered to her. The baby stopped when she came to Philosopher and Skeptic and curled up between them. They didn't know whether to move away, or allow the little animal to be so close to them. Skeptic looked at her with open repulsion. Philosopher hesitatingly touched her head and she promptly fell sleep.

Gently placing the little bird into her lap, the new arrival said, "I'll introduce my hen later." She gestured to her magnificent vehicle (*I think she addressed him as "Thomas"*) and suggested he find something to eat and drink and return when he was refreshed. The giant started to move gracefully out of the clearing.

"Wait!" Darwin shouted. "May I go with him? I never imagined any animal would evolve into a beast as remarkable as this."

The colossus swung around to face the man. Some of the monkeys sitting in the trees leaped out of his horns' way just in time. I don't think he liked being called a "beast." Galaxies swirled in his enormous eyes. They seemed to be in a Universe all their own. The Evolutionist was taken aback by the incredible spectacle and covered his face.

What now? The bushes encircling the clearing exploded into fire! The flames started to sway, and shifted into shapes of a myriad of bulls struggling in distress. Their shadows grew and covered the trees and cliffs. We could see many hanging by one hind leg choking on their own blood as it streamed from their throats. Throats that had been slit by men. Men obeying their ancient religion's law that has been on the books for thousands of years. Something about God and sacrifice and the proper preparation of meat.

We were not to be released from the horror unfolding before us. Someone next to me vomited as shadows of men in capes thrust long picks into the neck of an already traumatized bull. We heard a thunderous roar of what must have been a crowd of thousands screaming. Screaming for the death of courage and magnificence.

Then *Show Time*! The flames became the shape of a bull twisting his body into the air trying to shake off the pain caused by the "hot shot" electric prod stuck into his ass. The man on his back holds on to set a new record. Bull is terrified. Ride 'em high, boys! Yippee high high yay!

Blood red flames rose above the canopy. I thought we would be burned alive. The bulls' agonized screeching lasted for the longest seconds ever recorded in time. The sound of their torment shook the trees, rumbled the rocks, knocked me over. The animals in the forest disappeared into the dark. The sound of the outcry was all too familiar. They had to leave to be safe. Safe from us.

As quickly as they came, the flames shut down. Not a blade of grass was singed. It was as if nothing had happened. The stars reappeared indifferent, cold. Darwin was sobbing. He walked up to Thomas, lowered his head and fell to his knees. He stretched his arms onto the ground as far as they could go and placed his face in the dirt in deepest supplication. The light in Bull's eyes softened. The giant dropped to his knees too, and spread out his enormous front legs until his hooves touched the naturalist's outstretched fingertips. Somehow, one head touched the other. It was the most wondrous bow that ever was.

I looked up to see an endless line of cattle slowly walking up a ramp that stretched across the cosmos to some distant planet. Where were they going? I didn't want to know. I knew.

The magnificent Bull rose and stood on his back hind legs and walked around the circle looking down at each and every one of us directly in the eyes. He appeared to be half man, half bull. He looked toward his companion as if to ask, "How am I doing?" She smiled. With that, he assumed his position as the four-legged being he was. Darwin reached up to touch him. Bull was clearly annoyed at the man's arrogance. He shuddered and allowed his touch. The two left the clearing together. Not a leaf stirred. It was as if the moment had never taken place. I looked into Humanity's eyes. She looked away.

The newest visitor looked around the circle for a rock to sit on. I swear the rocks were competing to be her seat. The rock she chose formed a back for her to lean against. Not noticing, she leaned forward, hands gently cupping her little hen and stared at the fire. Without looking at any of us, she said, "I'm autistic. I understand how Thomas felt when Dr. Darwin touched him. Autistic people cannot tolerate being touched. I've learned that most food animals react the same way when they are handled inconsiderately. Thomas is a complex being. If he decides to, he'll reveal his true self to you. I think allowing Darwin's touch revealed something about Thomas's true nature. Whether he realized it or not, Dr. Darwin demonstrated that he believed himself to be superior to my traveling companion. Thomas figured that out right away, but his wisdom and maturity sloughed it off. Lucky for Darwin that he did."

She paused and gently stroked her little bird. It was shocking to see how frail and weak the featherless Chicken was. "This is an egg-laying hen. Most consumers don't know how rough it is for the egg-layers during their short lives. Although the factory farms have good publicists who make sure the public sees clean, humane conditions, it just isn't typically so. I've witnessed many kinds of atrocities. I remember the day I went to a chicken plant and found live chickens in various stages of dying stacked up in a garbage can. I was horrified.

"Every day, thousands of live chicks, mostly males, are trashed. Males can't lay eggs, so what good are they to the egg industry? In a plant owned by the largest distributor of chicken parts, I witnessed the workers killing the chickens by smashing them against the wall. It was awful."

She looked fondly at her little friend. "I think I'd rather be tossed in a garbage bin than be one of the female chickens forced to lay up to two-hundred fifty eggs before her body gives out." Looking across the circle without looking into the eyes of anyone in particular, she continued, "I've heard that the hens go insane within a matter of two days because of the horrid conditions they are placed in. Wouldn't you? Their beaks must be removed so they won't harm each other. When they can lay no more, their fragile bodies are quite depleted. They can't be used for anything other than in foods with labels that say they contain 'chicken products.' Many of my students have proudly told me they've stopped eating beef and pork, but still eat chicken. They ask me, 'Eating chicken isn't eating meat, is it?'"

The Scientist's eyes turned dark. She was mad. It was the kind of mad that is sad around the edges. The kind of mad that occurs when people become frustrated when they can't do something about a bad situation. I started to worry. Would Sanctuary react to the dark mood we were sinking into? Not a cloud filled the skies.

She said, "I believe that the plant where a food animal is slaughtered is a sacred one. I'd like to see some sort of ritual be performed before the animals are brought in to the cutting room. It would serve as a means to shape the workers' behavior. The ritual could be something very simple. Maybe a moment of silence. No words. Just one pure moment of silence. I can picture it perfectly. It would help the workers from becoming numb, callous, and cruel during the kills. I'd like to see the ritual performed throughout the day in every slaughtering plant (aka: 'meat processing' plant)." We sat quietly for a few minutes, thinking about her wonderful idea.

Disrupting our silence, Temple said, "There's so much more I could tell you, but I'm not sure you can tolerate the stories without being upset. I remember watching a guy take an electric prod and shove it down a cow's throat just for plain meanness. Another time, I saw a man shoot out a cow's eyes before the animal began its trip down the line! There are sadists working in the slaughter plants who are overlooked or ignored by the management."

That did it! The group exploded into rage. The illusion of neutrality in Sanctuary ended. Sanctuary's atmosphere began to react to our inability to keep peace. The temperature started to rise.

Animal Communicator shouted through the din, "Please don't fight! The food animals want you to know that they choose to come back into bodies that will feed others to experience every life form. It's just that they are disappointed when their treatment is so rough."

Skeptic is heated. "Communicator! I can't believe a thing you are saying! You are a very imaginative person to come up with such a fantastic story. Who do you think you are? Who empowered you to tell us what's on the animals' minds?"

Communicator began to cry. "All I know is that I can hear the animals' thoughts. They come to me!"

Skeptic stomp-walked over to her and yelled in her face, "Their thoughts come to you? Well, this has come to me! None of your discussion has had any scientific value. Let alone made sense!"

Someone sided with Skeptic, another with Communicator. The winds entered the fray. If we calmed down, the winds calmed. If we grew agitated, they increased in velocity. An angry Guardian stalked Cleric around the circle. When he caught up with him, he shook him hard. Healer shouted, *"No! No! This is not the way!"* The ground shifted and began to shake. The animals backed away from us.

The shouting became deafening. Someone cried, "Stop! We're out of control! I'm afraid! *Stop now!*" A biophony of strange sounds filled Sanctuary. The trees had become willing instruments for the winds to play a haunting dirge. Somehow I knew it was for us. Sanctuary turned dark. The air became heavy, dense. I couldn't catch my breath. A monstrous storm produced lightning strikes just above our heads. The wind's power was strengthened by our terrified screams, and easily broke the trunks of many giant trees. So much for musical trees.

The ancient forest's canopy roof ripped open to reveal the blackest of black outer space. What happened to the stars and galaxies? Is Sanctuary changing its orbit? Where are we going? Clouds of flying debris swarmed through the forest and spiraled upward into the skies. Deep crevices opened up. Steam rose from the Sea and immediately froze into hellish red clouds that hovered just above the crowd. A tree branch crashed down knocking me out. When I woke up, my mouth was bleeding and I was sore all over. No time to find out how injured I was.

I wondered whether (Sea) Guardian were safe. We hadn't seen him since he joined the animals in that water funnel so long ago. He later related that the ocean became a maelstrom filled with sea dwellers. He was sucked to the bottom and battered by their dead bodies. The sea animals fought for their lives. Many were drowned by the upheaval we had started on land.

I sat up and watched in horror as the forms of the Universal Images began to vibrate slowly, then shook violently into every possible contortion and twist. Are they in pain? Their now transparent bodies shifted into the exotic colors of the cosmic skies. The colors had become electric neon and hurt my eyes.

At first, the human forms emerged from their single iconic selves frame by frame as if in a slow motion film. Without warning, dozens of people contained within their particular Universal Image flew up and out of their icon until the body they occupied became a blur. One by one, the Universal Images representing the most brilliant and respected people on Earth became empty of substance.

Rising out of one of the forms were the same Light Beings I saw merge into the body of Scientist on that sleepless night before the day of our first meeting. On that wondrous occasion, I witnessed the enjoining of great souls-in-common who came together for a noble cause. Now, in this horrific scene, the personas within Scientist were pulling out fast! It was chaos. Awesome chaos.

Sanctuary became crowded with a multitude of human beings battering each other. Screaming in high pitch, every person claimed to know the answer to the animals' question. Some were able to remember why they were here in the first place and pleaded to the animals for help. Most were too busy getting away from each other to think about the animals. *Animal-human spiritual connection*? Impossible! Humanity simply vanished in a puff.

The Teachers were hysterical. In spite of myself, I chuckled when I saw two of them slapping each other's faces over and over again. "I'm right!" (Slap.) "No, I'm right!" (Slap slap!) Something about their action reminded me of me, and I stopped laughing. Dozens of Guardians ran after the Teachers. I couldn't understand why, but guessed they had their reasons.

Transparent yet distinguishable, a renowned Philosopher emerged from his Universal Image punching another in the nose. The other was swinging back awkwardly punching the air.

Countless heroic figures shot out and away from their respective Universal body without so much as a passing glance. Arms extending upward, new spiritual thinkers flew out of their respective Universal form. Some emerged from Cleric, some from Philosopher, some from Sage. Unfettered by rigid ideas held by religions, they easily broke free. I recognized Rudolph Steiner, Annie Besant, Edgar Cayce, Regina Hyland, Michael Roads,

Gangaji, and Jane Roberts arm in arm with Seth soar into the skies. I thought of ashes of burning leaves rising from a bonfire. First sparking into the dark night, then gone. It was as if they never were.

The Universal Image of Cleric became a grotesque, amorphous blob with hundreds of tentacles waving wildly. Looking closer, I could see each tentacle tip had become a head of a spiritual advisor. Rabbis, ministers, priests, popes, mullahs, gurus, shamans and every other self-proclaimed representative of a religion were screaming for help from their god – goddess – God. Their hysterical screeching was at ear-splitting pitch.

Two rabbis grasped their hands around each other's throats. One shouted, "*Deuteronomy 12! You may slaughter and eat meat . . . But do not partake of the blood – for the blood is the life. You must not consume the life (blood) with the flesh!*" The other screamed "*Isaiah 66:3! Those who slaughter oxen and slay humans, who sacrifice sheep and immolate dogs . . . so will I choose to mock them . . .They did what I deem evil and chose what I do not want!*"

A pope had the head of a mullah in his mouth while another mullah chewed on the pope's tentacle. One was gnawing on himself. Aristotle laughed at the sight until he choked and disappeared entirely. The Clerics struggled to break away from the awesome body they were attached to. For a moment, I thought I saw the great Bull emerge out of Thomas Aquinas's front side. Both of their mouths were full of straw. It was garbled, but I'm sure I heard Thomas shout before the awful blob moved on, "Everything I have written is straw!" I spotted Raven struggling to stay upright in the now hurricane force, shouting to Thomas, "You know! You really know!"

The blob that once was Cleric began to expand until it filled the clearing. The robes worn by those clerics who stood between their followers and their God shredded and fell away. The pages of the holy books they clutched tore off page by page and were tossed into the storm. Without their trappings, not one religion's representative was discernable from another. Thankfully, Cleric's tentacles withdrew and were no more.

It got worse. The Universal Image of Cleric became one cavernous mouth that began to consume everything in sight. In one noisy gulp, the orifice swallowed what was left of the forest.

The animals stampeded or flew away just in time and found refuge in the cliff caves. The seas sloshed as if they were in a giant bowl. Waves tumbled onto shore in an attempt to throw water on the heat of our violent anger. The sea formed a gargantuan funnel for a second time. I froze as the massive, whirling shape left the waters. It moved across the land, vacuuming up everything in sight. No one escaped. Cleric was taken whole.

My knees buckled. I fell to the ground and grabbed onto a root hoping it would hold as the funnel closed in on me. The last thing I saw was Guardian straining to grab Change Maker's foot as she rose into the funnel. He missed and she spun off. Another and another were lifted up and tossed into the abyss. I howled, "Wait for me! Don't leave me here! I'm afraid! So afraid! So afraid! *Please take me with you!*" The winds absorbed my shrieks with howls of their own. Lightning blasted across the atmosphere.

MIRACULOUSLY, THE STORM STOPPED. The debris tossing in the skies and on the ground has begun to glitter! Bits now reduced to fragments of bits have become shiny little mirrors reflecting what had been Sanctuary. The bits shattered into smaller bits still reflecting what had been. The smaller bits broke into even smaller pieces again and again until I could no longer see them. I imagined they were microscopic in size, and getting smaller than that. The bitty bitty bits swirled together into colorful, complex geometric patterns. Each pattern folded into more amazing patterns as if some master weaver were conducting an orchestra gone mad. The flow moved across the ground, absorbing and transforming every thing it touches. Sanctuary is reorganizing into one continuous, marvelous fractal state! Paralyzed in fear and awe, I witnessed a phenomenon never before seen in the Universe.

Then, as if someone snapped its fingers, everything was gone! No skies, no ground, no trees, no seas, no life, no fractal flow. Airless, lightless, nothingness. Sanctuary came from nothing. Now it has returned to nothing. Am I nothing too? No such luck. I'm still here. Where is here? What will happen to me? Maybe it's already happened to me. Maybe I am one of the bits flowing into the flow and am incapable of comprehending it. Is this what death feels like? Maybe I am dead. If I'm not dead, I want to die.

The root I'd been clinging to snapped and thrust me into the dense blackness of the abyss. It's so cold! Where am I? Where is Sanctuary? Where have all the humans gone? Where are the other animals? Have we separated so completely from Nature and each other that our end is the abyss? Are we traveling to some sort of Hell because we refuse to accept the truth about ourselves? I tried to scream. If I have made a sound, I can't hear it. I am alone!

In complete terror, I lose consciousness.

ACT 3

THAT THEY COME INTO THEIR OWN

ELEVEN
Restoration

I'M FLOATING IN SOME SORT OF BUBBLE. Bubble? Where am I? My knees are bent under my chin. My arms wrapped around my knees. I sleep like this most of the time at home curled up in a corner of my bed. If I ever get back, I'll never leave my bed, my private bed. My heart is beating wildly. Can hardly breathe. I stretch my arms as far as I can and touch a soft, moist wall. At least it's warm in here.

Now I remember. They're gone! The people, the animals are gone! Am I gone? What about the animals? I failed them. What was I thinking? My prideful ego convinced me I could do anything I set my mind to do. Who do I think I am? What made me think I could pull it off? Save the animals? I couldn't save myself let alone those wonderful, gentle beings who believed in me. That's the worst part. The animals trusted me. They trusted all of us. We failed. I failed. Utterly failed. Will the Universe forgive me?

A few squabbles turned into out of control anger and destruction. We broke a simple law: *There will be no dissension in Sanctuary*. Now we'll never know the answer to the animals' question. We couldn't escape our own selves, and reverted to what we were when we started. We selfishly killed the dream and took our lives in the process. Humankind? Where did that term come from? Humans aren't kind to themselves let alone the other animals. O God! I want to scream, cry, find something to tear my heart out! Our grand intention blew up and shattered Sanctuary along with everything else. Just let me die! Please let me die?

Can't seem to keep my eyes open . . .

I awaken. Still in this "place." God help me! I'll be good. I'll

109

think only sweet, kind thoughts about every person I meet (if I ever meet another person). I'll dedicate every waking moment to serving You, God. I promise I will never be arrogant or upset by petty things. I will trust You and only You.

Sleepy, so sleepy . . .

Awake again. How am I going to get out of here? I'll clear my head by meditating. That's what I'll do! Ommm. *Ommm!* But what if I'm stuck in here forever? *Omm!* For eternity? *Ommmm!* Is this eternity? *Ommmmm!* Is this all there is? *Hey, God!* I'm talking to you! Don't I deserve some sort of sign or answer? *Om . . .* Omm? Look at all that I've done for the animals! At least I tried to help them find the answer to their question. Don't I deserve some credit for that?

Eyelids are heavy. Sinking into sweet sleep . . .

Awake once more. What time is it? What day is it? I'm getting used to this fluid-filled enclosure. Floating can be pleasantly relaxing. No people to answer to. No animals to worry about. It's nice being in here with me. Just me. I'm safe with me.

Here I go again! Why can't I dream?

Awake again. Am I still here? Where is here? Oh, God!!? Where are you? Maybe I'm in Hell. Is this the Hell my Sunday school teacher told me I'd go if I didn't learn the books of the Bible in their correct order? Genesis, Exodus, Leviticus, Numbers, Psalms. No, that's not right. What book comes after Numbers? I can't seem to concentrate.

"What is your problem?" my inner voice asks. I answer myself rudely, *"I'm trapped in a warm, slimy bubble and can't get out! That's my problem!"* When I opened my mouth, the liquid flowed in and choked me. I coughed and coughed until I was exhausted. I nearly drowned. Drowned?

Sleep. Blessed sleep.

Awake once more. Not a thought in my head. I searched my mind. Nothing. It's empty. I'm empty-headed. I laugh at my joke. At least I didn't choke this time. I snapped my mouth shut. Better not take any chances.

Now what? I'm in some kind of a tunnel. Can barely fit. Every few seconds I'm being thrust toward an opening. I hear screams! The screams are dreadful. Howling! Angry howling. Push! The sounds are getting louder. Push! Cheers! Thrust! Scream! Push, thrust, push! Someone is grabbing my head. Ow! Push! Owww! The light is too bright! Turn off the light! *Owwwww!*

I'm out of my bubble! Where am I? So tired. So tired . . .

How long have I been lying here? I can move my legs! I am able to stand up! Phew! What is that awful smell? Where did all this garbage come from? Newspapers, plastic containers, metal cans, rotting vegetables and stinking fruits cover the ground. Some of the waste is piled in great mounds. It's difficult to walk through the ooze. Every step is a test of balance. I don't want to fall into the slimy stuff.

Even with all the rubble, I know this is Sanctuary. Tears fill my eyes. Sanctuary has returned, but at what cost? A mysterious red atmosphere has replaced the magnificent skies. Avalanches have split boulders from the cliffs. Forms of giant beings are frozen in some sort of twisted dance. Parts of the forest remain, but the trees are leafless, dead. The exposed sea floor is most disturbing. Thousands of species of fish and sea mammals are dead. Many are still foundering in a vast wasteland of sludge. The stench of their bodies is sickening. What have we done? Maybe deep inside we chose to destroy Sanctuary rather than face the knowing. As usual, Sanctuary complied. I'd give anything to see Secret again. He knows what we know. What we knew. Gratefully, I found an old pair of shoes sticking out of the sludge. They fit! I could walk in the muck without getting my bare feet cut by the broken glass buried in the ooze. I walked for hours searching for some sign of life. Crying the whole way, I begged Sanctuary. Called to the Universe! Pleaded with the elementals! Shouted at God! Wailed at nothing in particular. "Help me somebody! Anybody? Help me!"

Chilled to the bone, I shivered uncontrollably. A white (at least I think it had been white) robe was sticking out of a particularly disgusting mound of mold. Tugging hard, I finally pulled it out. As I decided whether to put it on or not, a clear pool appeared nearby. The water was warmer than the air yet refreshingly cool enough to drink. After swishing the garment in the water to loosen some of the crud, I put it on. It warmed me in spite of its dampness.

A strange light rose slowly above the horizon exaggerating the shapes of the broken trees, the piles of stinking debris and those enormous rocks. The light distorts the landscape into grotesque shadows that crisscross the ground surface. As I walked, I saw them! There were people out there! I ran toward them, but stopped abruptly. A crowd of strangers walked toward me silently with their arms stretched out in front of them. They passed me by inches. Why couldn't they see each other or me? Were they blind? No one spoke. If they would only speak to each other, they would make their passage easier. Maybe they're afraid to try. I started to call to them but they disappeared into one of the greater shadows.

I waited several minutes hoping the people would return. I needed their company. Yet, I had a feeling that if I went into that shadow, I'd disappear too. When I turned around from the dark shadow where they had gone, the light on the horizon brightened and warmed the air. Warmed my spirit.

What? Do my eyes deceive me? The Universal Images are back! There's Skeptic and Teacher chatting amicably. Change Maker and Guardian have found each other and are walking toward me hand in hand! And, yes! Healer and Communicator are heading this way. With the arrival of each Universal Image, the skies grew brighter. The light cleared the air and dissipated that suffocating red atmosphere.

A lone figure walked toward us. He picked up an empty can and shoved it in his backpack. Again and again, he bent over and added another piece of garbage to his pack. It's Scientist! Science survived! I ran toward him with my arms wide open for a big hug. Mistake. He shimmered and faded away. I turned and ran to Change Maker and Guardian. They too faded. *"No! No! No!"* I screamed, fell to my knees and raised my hands to the skies. "I give up! I can't do this anymore! You (whoever you are) win!"

I don't know how long I lay curled up on the ground with eyes tightly shut, fists clenched. I finally looked up when I heard a bird chirping. It was the sweetest sound ever to be heard anywhere in the Universe. The animals are back! What's this? A sprout of green is growing between two rocks! I've never seen anything so beautiful as this lone sprout. Its fresh smell cleansed the air around it. I sat up to see grasses and plants sprouting up and out from the garbage. Wonderful! Foliage is covering the debris.

Some of the Universal Images were looking down at me. One grasped my hand and pulled me up to stand. We walked until we found our clearing where we'd spent so many days and formed our familiar circle. We sat quietly as we always did before our meetings. I leaned over to touch Philosopher, but my hands passed through her body. This time I was able to accept the fact that she was not real. Simply an image. A Universal Image of Philosophers everywhere.

"Kwork!" Raven is back! The giant black bird shyly hopped to Skeptic and dropped one of his tail feathers in front of him. Smiling broadly, Skeptic gently picked it up and put it behind his ear and said, "I thought long and hard about Raven while floating out there in that infernal bubble. So much so that he has been coming into my dreams lately." Skeptic was perplexed by his own words. "Thinking about that bird? In my dreams, too?"

A look of relief came across his face. "He did his best to annoy me. Now I know Raven had a job to do. This marvelous being taught me to accept all the probabilities about him and the other animals I'd closed my mind about." Skeptic dropped his head and said, "With every fiber of my being I repent to the dogs and other animals for my insane egotism. I wanted a little notoriety in my times and got it at their expense."

He walked from animal to animal, knelt in front of them, and offered his hand. "I must know," he said looking into the eyes of every animal. "Will you forgive me for my self-righteousness," humbly looking down, "and cruelty?"

Tails wagged, tongues licked, paws touched him. We are not the people we were when we first arrived in Sanctuary. We have changed and the animals know.

Skeptic said, "When I return to my times I will rescind my falsified experiments, and teach the true nature of the other animals." He looked lovingly at Raven who was busy preening himself. The other animals don't hesitate to scratch an itch or preen a preen no matter what the situation is. I'm sure Raven appreciated Skeptic's overture. It's just that preening can't wait.

Raven looked lovingly at Skeptic. His ebony body began to

glow. The light came from his feathers, beak and eyes. I didn't know whether to be afraid or thrilled by the sight. When the light withdrew, he hopped onto Skeptic's outstretched hand. Skeptic placed him on his shoulder and from that moment on they were inseparable. They would stay together for centuries.

An exaltation of Larks flew out of the forest and circled over our heads. One landed on Healer's shoulder, one on Scientist's knee, and two on Cleric's outstretched hands. They were about to settle in when Cat suddenly dashed into the circle obviously hoping to startle the Larks and us. Cat is amused. We're not. The birds squawked an unlark-like sound and flew to safer heights in the trees. Heights? Trees? We looked up to see the canopy restored. Galaxies spiral across the cosmos just above the forest. Welcome back, Sanctuary! Welcome back, celestial skies!

A giggle came from the hollow of one of the older trees. It was Secret! He smiled broadly and rump first, slowly lowered himself to the ground. His emergence from the tree was awkward to say the least. "Well," he said. "You sure made a mess of things! You couldn't even figure out who I am. You came close but not quite close enough. It's time for me to introduce myself properly, and reveal the 'mysterious' Secret you've anguished over."

The shabby, drab cloak he wore when he first appeared to us was now brightly multi-colored. The hood was gone, and we could see his face. His (or her) face was androgynous, childlike, angelic. If we were to guess his gender, we wouldn't be able to come to an agreement. Didn't matter. Gender is not part of the discussion. It is simply a form of self-identification while we are in physical body along with our ethnicity, skin color, and all the other characteristics we humans use to assess each other. We were very glad to see him again. He belonged here with us.

Secret walked into the center of our circle and sat on the ground with his legs crossed. His hands rested palms up on his knees. No matter where we were sitting it seemed he was looking directly into our own eyes as he spoke. His voice changed, became ethereal in tone. "You wonder who I am? Let me explain. I am the caretaker of your secrets." How could he know our most hidden thoughts? I searched my mind trying to ferret out the secrets I keep inside me. Secrets that could hurt me if they were known. Things I couldn't bear if anyone knew.

Secret seemed to be reading our minds, and looked around the circle. "I'm not here to reveal your personal secrets." There was a collective sigh of relief. "There is a much greater, awesome Secret that is hidden within every (and I mean every) human being on Earth whether she is a CEO of a worldwide corporation, or he is stalking a monkey in a rain forest to feed his hungry family. Every human being on Earth is born with this universal Secret! Imagine! Even you, the personas contained within Universal Images of the highest rank, are keeping the same Secret from each other." We looked at each other. Some openly showed their confusion. I was lost.

"I was able to live in you because you didn't know I was there. It was easy for me to stay hidden because you were quite busy keeping your other little secrets from each other and the rest of the people in your lives. Those of you who might have had an inkling of my presence hoped you'd hidden me so well that even your God wouldn't find me. This is ironic because the great Secret I am about to reveal concerns your own true self in relationship with all that exists. This Secret makes all your other secrets puny and worthless. Certainly, not of any importance to you."

"What?" Teacher asked. "How is this possible? How can every human being be keeping the same secret? It's some sort of trick!"

Ignoring the challenge, Secret said, "This is an historic moment for us all! You are about to receive the hidden knowledge the peoples of the Earth could not (or would not) face until now. Once you fully and completely accept the Secret, you will be set free." We looked at each other. What did Secret mean by setting us free?

"There's more. As long as we are in Sanctuary, you will appear to the group in the form of your assigned Universal Image. Your real job is beginning right now! Once your work is completed in Sanctuary, the individuals you represent will return to their own times to share what they've learned. Any questions?" I had many but decided to wait and see. The rest of the group had none.

"First, dear Universal Images," he grinned, "Congratulations! Coming to Sanctuary was probably the most difficult task ever undertaken by so many renowned people. Every person courageously and selflessly accepted the animals' challenge, and joined with like-minded others to embody one of ten Universal Images." Turning to Humanity he said, "You're in a class all by yourself, great Mother."

Humanity looked puzzled, but said nothing. "All of you (*bowing to Humanity*) came to Sanctuary to find the answer to the animals' question, '*What happened to the animal-human spiritual connection?*' As the days went by, you learned that the animals' question set many other questions into motion."

Taking a deep breath, Secret stood up and started to pace. A look of doubt swept across his face. As if hearing encouragement from somewhere out there, he continued with confidence. "From the beginning times when you settled on Earth, you created a grand misconception about yourselves and integrated that belief into every aspect of your politics, laws, arts, sciences, philosophies and religions.

"Either you misunderstood or you chose to ignore the truth about who you really are. For that matter, you denied the truth about your relationship with the Universe itself. You spend your time on Earth separating yourselves from all that exists around you. Even the texts of your religions strengthen the position of superiority you give yourselves over and above the other animals and the Earth itself. The original sin you banter about in some world religions has nothing to do with banishment from Eden over a bite of an apple.

"If there is such a thing as 'sin,' the original sin is believing you are separate from everything and everyone else. The mistake you continue to make is believing that separation from others is even possible," he said. I've heard these words spoken by many spiritual teachers and found them in their texts, but could not envision how they applied to me. Now I think I do.

Two baby chimpanzees began to play tag on a tree branch above us. Secret was forced to raise his voice to be heard. Their ruckus called for stronger measures. He found a gnarled stick lying close by and gently tapped it on the tree trunk. They immediately settled down. Good thing. Secret wasn't in the mood for play.

"By denying your true Self, you have struggled every step of the way. Don't you see? It's been difficult to continue the charade of separation. It meant you had to cut off your connection with each other and the Earth itself. By separating from each other you were forced to learn how to survive alone . . . then forgot who you truly are.

"Think about it. Your innermost secret beliefs revolve around matters that pertain to your relationships with others. The consequences of holding onto such beliefs were shown to you when you were thrown into the abyss. You needed a 'time out' after you destroyed Sanctuary with your out-of-control emotions. You were isolated in your bubbles and would still be there if you hadn't come to realize that your behavior affects every one and every thing around you."

He turned to the two most divisive of the Universal Images and dramatically waved his stick at them. "Scientist! Cleric! You have betrayed the people you represent." Surprised, both looked up. "Scientists and religionists have much in common. It requires imagination and stubborn perseverance to initiate and carry out the ideas that have shaped your disciplines. Rather than working together, you choose to spend most of your time trying to prove the other wrong.

"Scientific versus religious beliefs is a popular debate that possibly will never be settled. You secretly know your two worldviews cancel each other out. Because of your arrogance you have blocked the next evolutionary step for all life." Secret paused to watch a flock of snow geese passing over us. They shouted their affirmation of the truth he had just revealed. Secret bowed and waved.

"Scientist, throughout history you have spent lifetimes trying to find what causes 'life' by dissecting the parts of every life form you can find. Here we are in the twenty-first century and you still can't explain how a newborn animal takes its first breath, can you? Now you are seeking the origin of your existence beyond the Earth itself. Lately you've been wondering whether 'life' as you know it began somewhere in the stars. Few scientists have ever looked for the answers within themselves."

Scientist was bewildered. "I have no idea what he is talking about," he whispered to Goat who was standing by chomping on a lovely batch of grasses. Goat didn't either.

Secret continued, "Don't get me wrong, Scientist. Your work has greatly improved the human condition. Your discoveries have conquered diseases, expanded knowledge of the physical world, and inspired technologies that will allow you to travel further into the cosmos. Maybe into time itself. You produce glorious images of the Universe to share with the public. Your conjectures about the Universe are stretching people's understanding of the cosmos. But, please don't ignore the dark side of your work, Scientist. The losses to other animals 'sacrificed' in your laboratories for the common (human) good are staggering.

"Probably your greatest strength is your greatest weakness. Your working premise, 'Unless you can see or measure it, it doesn't exist' is quite primitive. No matter how sophisticated your technologies are, you will never find the answers to your questions as long as you stay within your traditional parameters."

Secret walked over to where Scientist was seated, and stood in front of him, arms folded. "My friend, countless unseen, immeasurable unknowns exist that far surpass any possible hypotheses you can imagine." We looked at Scientist to get his reaction. He was distracted by a new genus of Dragonfly that had landed on Secret's shoulder. When it flew away, he ran after the elusive insect shouting, "Be right back! Go on without me!"

Unperturbed, Secret turned to Cleric. "Cleric, throughout history many of you exploited, tortured and conquered large populations in the name of your God. You continue to threaten terrible consequences (a hellish afterlife or reincarnating into a hellish life on Earth) if your devotees don't follow *your* interpretation of the ancient wisdoms. With such dreadful standards, people have backed away not only from your religions but also away from the wonders of the unknown. Many have simply shut down.

"You tell us that you have been 'called by God' to speak for your religion. Many of you put yourselves on a pedestal so high that even the God you profess can't reach you."

(*Secret paused long seconds.*) "I must say my statement isn't entirely true. Thousands of Clerics serve people and animals all over the world, whether the people they help are followers of the Clerics' religion or not." For the first time, Cleric was at a loss for words.

Secret began to sway. We swayed with him. This time, we (almost) knew! He froze mid-step in his dance. He'd noticed some of us didn't follow what he was saying. I was one of them. His voice softened. "I can't blame you for not understanding what I'm trying to say. You can't blame yourself. It can be terrifying believing you are separate from every thing and every one else. Think of it this way . . .

"Starting in your infancy, you were conditioned to protect your physical body. As soon as you stubbed your toe or sipped a very hot spoonful of soup, you became painfully aware of your physical separation from that hard wall and that soup. You developed an awareness of your body first. Next, you took your separate body out into the world and soon found you must hone your individual persona-character to fit in with the crowd."

Secret paused and shook his head. "How difficult it must be for you! You are reminded constantly that you are separate from every thing and every one you encounter! While in physical form, your reality is the smell of coffee brewing, taking a hot shower, that pain in your toe. You turn on the TV to watch reports about casualties in wars, about a horse drowning in a flood and a family lost in an avalanche. You think you are separate from the troubles of those people and the horse. After all, you were not killed in that war or drowned or lost your family." I looked over to check Humanity's reaction to what we were hearing. She seemed to be ignoring Secret. The energies flowing beneath her skin were calm.

Secret was still talking. "What if I told you that you are not only experiencing what is happening around you, you *are* the experiences? Listen to me!" Humanity looked up. "You *are* the smell of the coffee, the water cleansing you, the hard surface where you stubbed your toe. You believe you are separate from everybody else as if they were performing for you in one big television 'reality show' to be watched from a distance. Can't you see it was *you* who was wounded in that war, drowned in that flood and lost in that mountain of snow?"

He paused. "I've got a news flash for you! There is an awesome reality waiting for you when you are able to accept what I am saying." Secret smiled and gestured toward the animals. "The other animals live in this reality. They sense everything around them. You call their intelligence 'instinct.' The animals' abilities are much more. Without the emotional baggage you carry, the other animals are fully aware of the pure essence of Nature. They see, hear, and feel the earth moving, the waters flowing. They sense every detail of the moment and never question their place in it. The animals not only exist within Nature, they *are* Nature.

"It's as if humans live in a parallel Universe with their own set of rules. Nature has been replaced by the code of the cultures you live in. You have been taught to behave toward people and other animals as your particular society expects you to behave. This can be confusing when in reality you belong to every society on earth."

Scientist rejoined the meeting without his specimen. Dragonfly will live for another day.

Secret's shoulders appeared to droop. He seemed to be growing old before our eyes. His eyes filled with tears. I knew he was feeling sorry for us. I felt sorry for us too. He pulled a handkerchief from his pocket and blew his nose. His blowing was more of a high-pitched toot. Apparently, he hadn't gotten the hang of nose blowing since his physical form was simply a figment of his and our imagination. If only I could get my mind off stubbing my toe.

Secret wasn't finished. "Your reality is limited to what you see, hear, taste, smell and touch in the material world. It's an old saying, but it works here. 'You can't see the forest for the trees.'"

Just then, a leaf fell into my lap. The Tree I sat under had delivered a part of itself to me. I silently thanked the Tree and looked up to see a wisp of smoke threading Tree's branches to the other Tree branches. Across the canopy as far as I could see, a translucent web of light-filled smoke connected the trees. The Forest shimmered! The effect was breathtaking. I glanced around the clearing hoping similar threads were linking us. If we were connected to each other, I wasn't able to see it.

I felt my head being stroked. Actually, I was feeling the strokes I was giving to Rabbit who was purring Rabbit purrs as she cuddled against me. I had to stifle purrs of my own. Then I looked up to see joy on the faces of the Universal Images and in the eyes of the animals. They too were experiencing the incredible gossamer web interconnecting every leaf, tree, branch and root in the Forest to us. Secret continued talking as if nothing were happening.

He stopped to scratch his backside with his stick and complained about the inconvenience of being in physical form. Made me itchy watching him. I scratched an itch. It was contagious. The others started scratching itches. Some helped others scratch the places they couldn't reach themselves. We looked around at the squirming bodies relieving themselves of a very physical need and laughed. Secret wasn't laughing, although he did stifle a grin. Time to get serious.

Secret asked the group to take a walk alone and in silence to think about what had been discussed. We were reluctant to leave each other. We had been taught a Universal truth and Forest revealed to us how it works. We returned to the circle in just a few minutes, and sat close together as one body, one mind.

Secret began again. "Denying what you know deep inside you is a form of ignore- ing. Ignoring becomes *Ignorance*. Denial of the obvious is conscious ignorance. Men of every culture and religion *know* (yet ignore) women are equal to them in the eyes of their god and should be treated with the same respect they give each other. Those who slaughter the food animals inefficiently *know* (yet ignore) the animals' struggles to break free from pain. Those who eat the animals *know* (yet ignore) that the animals suffered during their kill. Those who experiment on live animals *know* the animals are in terror, yet they ignore their cries. I could go on and on."

He lightly tapped his stick on Skeptic's shoulder. Raven had hopped into Skeptic's lap and was nuzzling his cheek. "Skeptic, you learned during your experiments that the other animals were not machines. You simply ignored the fact to prove your premise that they have no souls." Skeptic looked up and nodded.

Secret was pleased by Skeptic's affirmation and continued, "The governing powers in office of every nation on Earth know that war is not the answer to any disagreement they can come up with. In other words, every human being on the planet knows deep within their true selves there is no way they can separate from another life form. Whether it is at the physical level or the spiritual level. Only the Universe knows why humans have chosen to keep this truth secret."

Secret looked into the eyes of each of us and said, "Just days ago the animals and I watched in dismay as you, Universal

Images who were given form through conscious intention, found it impossible to tolerate each other. Let alone accept the very personas embodied in you. I am amazed you were given a reprieve and were allowed to come back to Sanctuary."

"*I knew it!*" shouted Cleric. "*God* gave us the reprieve!" Secret smiled gently at the Universal Image representing every religious thought ever thought. "I am speaking of the reprieve given to you by your own true self. When the individual personalities within your Universal image held onto their own personal beliefs, they descended into the same violence human beings have resorted to since they first walked on Earth." He began to pace. "Sanctuary reacted and well, you know what happened next." Secret's face was etched with lines made deep by his grief. "I don't have to tell you how awful your behavior was."

Secret chuckled at our sincere dismay. "Cheer up! You passed the test. When you realized why you were thrown into the abyss, you were able to return and restore what you destroyed. And you raised hope for me. I will be released from you when you no longer need to hide behind me anymore!" Secret danced a little jig of anticipation.

"Let me tell you a story about how we came to exist." Secret jumped onto a rock (no doubt to be seen by all of us), and began.

"*In the beginning, there was no one, no where. No light, no air. Picture sheer emptiness. Picture one infinite, vacuum-ous Void. Not idle, mind you, the Void was conscious of its only-ness. Its One-ness. You might say the One was conscious of itself. Whether the One planned it or not is unclear, but after a long, long, very long time, something happened that changed what was forever.*"

Secret checked every face to see if we were listening. (We were.) "*Without warning, (if anyone were around to warn anyone) a neutronic, invisible-to-the-naked-eye seed-particle appeared within the One.*"

Someone asked, "The seed was an extension of the One, right?" Either Secret didn't hear the question or didn't want to address it.

"*The seed didn't know what it was. Yet. Didn't know its names. Yet. In that darkest of darkness, the teeny weensy seed began to glow! The light grew brighter and brighter until the One could no longer hold that which was growing within. The first breath ever was breathed!*"

(Some say it was more like an astronomic, cosmic, multi-dimensional burp.)"

We moved in closer until we were sitting on the ground under the rock he was standing on. Secret loves a good audience. He raised his voice and waved his arms dramatically. *"The light-seed burst from its source with such energy that it ripped the infrastructure of the Void! In that incredible moment, the particle-seed illuminated the darkness of the infinite space as if it were lighting a small, dark room!"*

He held a finger over his lips and whispered, *"Next came soundless, silent stillness. You could hear a pin drop if there were a pin to drop."* He cupped his hand to his ear as if seeking the sound of a pin dropping.

Then he shouted so loudly that Robin fell out of a tree. The embarrassed bird fluttered and flew back onto the branch where he'd been listening with all his might.

"Void roared a thunderous roar. 'Who disturbs my hommm?' The impact of that terrifying roar ruptured, tore, and shattered the One along with its seed into gazillions of subatomic bits! Altered beyond repair, the One became every thing that is! And I mean, every thing that exists, including us!"

Secret looked down at his rapt audience. Speaking faster, *"Then – another atto-moment of silence. Or was it shock? Maybe it was a moment of anguish for the end of the One's halcyon days. No time for shock or mourning! In an instant we separated from each other. Screeching and howling, we catapulted at incalculable speed moving further and further away from the source from which we came. We traveled so fast that our itty-bitty bodies left streams of light in their wake. In our panic, we didn't think to turn around. If we had, we'd have noticed that our own light streams were the very paths that would guide us back home."*

He paused and with a tease in his eye said, "I'm thirsty. Can someone bring me a little water?" We looked at each other. How could he disrupt his story now? Gibbon jumped up and swung through the trees and returned faster than she'd ever swung before with a leaf filled with water. What an admirable athlete Gibbon is! Secret sipped slowly, enjoying every moment of our anticipation and continued,

"Without looking back from where we came, we sped away from the source of our very existence. Frantically we called out to each other.

But no one could hear anyone else. We were lost and alone in the abyss."

We looked at each other and shuddered. We were quite familiar with the abyss. Someone asked, "Why would any One in its right mind, in its perfectly peaceful state, want to break itself up and become the many?"

The storyteller grinned. *"Sometimes on a blue sky, trouble-free day like this day I know the answer."* We leaned forward to hear it. He spoke clearly, confidently. *"I am a seed bit of the One. So are you. So is Cat curled up over there. So are the Trees bending from the Wind out there. So is the Wind coming from some where. So is the cozy we feel right here. We never left."*

We looked around the circle at each other. What did the dissenters in our midst think? In unison, we turned to Skeptic. He smiled. "That makes sense," he said. We turned to Scientist. "Well, there's no empirical evidence that this is how our origin happened, but then there is no empirical evidence that our adventures in Sanctuary happened either," Scientist said.

"I concur with Skeptic."

TWELVE
Making the Connection

Polar Bear lumbered into the clearing and sat on her haunches. "Let me get this straight," she growled. (Growling was her "normal" voice.) "When that tiny seed produced by the Void exploded, it shattered into zillions of subatomic, invisible-to-the-naked-eye bits. We were among those bits. In the excitement of breaking away we didn't give the matter a second thought. We were free! There was so much to do! So many possibilities to explore!"

Bear stood up. I was struck by her massive size. She was magnificent! "Those of us who were first to arrive on Earth found its environment suited us perfectly. The air was pristine. The land and seas offered their abundance. We were equipped with unique bodies with specialized capabilities making it possible for us to survive in our new surroundings."

After gently licking her cubs tussling at her feet she continued, "To perpetuate our species, we learned how to reproduce offspring. Living on the Earth in the physical bodies we had become, we felt the pangs of hunger and had to take shelter when the weather got rough. We agreed early on to share the resources of the land and waters with each other. Some were to be eaten. Others were to eat them. The game of survival was played without anger or fear. It was just a game. Every animal understood the game's number one law *'Take from the Earth only what you need'* and we obeyed it."

Billy Jo stepped into the circle. He stooped down to pet one of the cubs, and politely asked Bear if he could continue her story. She nodded and deferred to the great ape. Still tussling all the way, her cubs followed her out of the clearing.

Billy Jo began. "After billions of years of evolving from

simple to complex life forms, we called on the Universe to shake things up, add a new twist to the game, bring in new players. More millions of years later, a new species arrived on our Earth. This one was different. The new animals were able to lift up their front legs somehow and walk on the two back ones. They were scrawny, two-legged creatures who were forced to cover themselves with the other animals' skins to protect their delicate hides.

"Many of us dreaded the new species. There was something about the way they behaved toward us that we didn't trust. At first we felt we were safe because we were stronger than they were, and could outrun them or fly away. No matter how leery we were of the change, we didn't question what was happening to our world. We had no choice but accept the newcomers.

"The humans had a great advantage over the other animals. Their first step was to make an ally of our feared enemy. They befriended Fire! They even brought Fire into their shelters! None of us could figure out how they could do this without being burned. We had no choice but to live within the limitations of our bodies. In time, Earth became the exclusive domain of humans. The game was over for us."

Scientist joined Billy Jo in center circle. It was good to see the two standing side by side. They had diverged from a common ancestor six million years ago. Just 1.6 percent of their genome separates them.

Placing his hand on Billy Jo's shoulder, Scientist said, "My friend, you described first humans accurately. They were indeed scrawny and quite helpless in the face of predators and the harsh environment. The process of evolution separated the human mammals from the other animals. Maybe Nature decided to even out the physical advantage the other animals had over humans by dramatically increasing the human brain size. As the homo species' brains evolved, their cerebral neocortex grew to be 90 percent of their brain volume. Let me explain?"

Scientist picked up a stick and drew a simplified diagram of a profile of a skull on the ground. He explained, "The brain is our most complex and misunderstood organ. It controls all our bodily functions and is the locus of our thinking. We could spend days discussing the many animal species' brains. It's a fascinating study! For the sake of brevity, I am limiting this discussion to the most fundamental parts in mammalian brains.

"Mammals are the only animals with 'triune' brains: the Reptilian Complex, the Limbic system and the Cerebral Neocortex. These three 'brains' function as one system." The Universal Image of Scientist stopped speaking. He was listening to one of the personas within him. "Charles Darwin just reminded me that 'the difference in mind between man and the higher animals, as great as it is, certainly is one of degree and not of kind." Scientist looked at the great apes. "Chimpanzee, Orangutan, Gibbon and Gorilla have demonstrated their advanced intellect many ways here in Sanctuary." The apes smiled broadly.

The Monkeys began to protest. Their screeches became a raucous din. We had to wait a few ear-splitting moments until they calmed down. Scientist said, "Yes! Yes, dear Monkeys, you too have advanced intelligence. We'll discuss the functions of the neocortex of each and every primate later. OK with you?" The Monkeys seemed to be satisfied and calmed down.

Continuing, "Each 'brain' has a purpose, and works in tandem with the entire brain." Pointing to a small "brain" he'd drawn at the base of the human skull, he said, "This brain first appeared in Dinosaurs. The 'Reptilian Complex' (or R-Complex) is found in snakes, reptiles and fish today. When a mammal needs an appropriate response to a dangerous situation, this brain might dominate the other two. Simply put, it is the source of our out-of-control anger and activates the 'fight or flight' fear responses when our survival is at risk."

Skeptic said, "I was in 'flight or fight' mode when we first arrived in Sanctuary." Several in the group murmured "Me too!"

Scientist drew a branch-shaped "brain" covering the Reptilian brain. "Located on top of the R-Complex and connected to the neocortex lie the structures of the Limbic system. Among many purposes, the Limbic structures enhance the ways we control (or not) our fear and anger, and intensify our feelings of pleasure like eating good food and sex. Sometimes called the 'old-mammalian brain,' the Limbic system appeared in the brains of the other mammals long before the homo species came on the scene.

"The Limbic system activates when a decision must be made requiring intelligent action. Remember when Cat spotted Bull

Snake yesterday? He wasn't sure whether to play with Snake or run away. To our relief, Cat decided to hide in the brush until Snake moved on. Their encounter would not have been an easy thing to watch."

Scientist drew the largest "brain" which covered the Limbic system. "The Cerebral Neocortex is the most recently evolved. The larger the mammal's cerebral neocortex, the greater the cognitive levels in complex speech, long-term memory and reasoning. The neocortex enables creative thought processing in humans, primates, elephants, dolphins and whales."

Scientist paused again. Another persona within Scientist was speaking to him. "Carl Sagan wants you to know how complicated the neocortex is. He says, 'That (the neocortex) is where matter is transformed into consciousness, possibly our judgments; (possibly) our moral knowledge of good and evil.' In other words, humans' enlarged neocortex allows us to reason more, imagine more, and often to our disadvantage, want more than the other mammals."

A high-pitched whistle followed by a series of clicks pierced the air and our ears. The sound came from somewhere over the Sea. Scientist's lesson abruptly ended. We ran to the seashore to see what was causing the commotion. Rocking to and fro, the most beautiful Dolphin I've ever seen was "standing" upright in the water.

"Sorry for the loud call, but I had to get your attention!" she said. Somehow Dolphin was forming words. Her speech sounded more like a motorbike rumble. Dolphin explained she would use lower frequency vocalizations so we could understand her. No need. It was as if she were "speaking" directly to our minds.

"Don't forget to include the water inhabitants in your discussion, Scientist!" she said. "We would have invited you to hold your meetings in Sanctuary's Sea but you can't stay under water for very long without artificial means. We pity you for that. At the same time we wish we could join you on land. Maybe we'll be able to join each other on both land and sea in several more millions of years," she laughed.

"We are listening to your conversation with mixed emotions. We can't understand why the animals that dwell in the largest biosphere on Earth are rarely mentioned in your discussions!

Earth's waters cover seventy percent of our planet's surface, and ninety-seven percent of that water is saltwater. Did you know that the ocean mid-waters are populated by more animal species than all of Earth's rainforests combined? I think these facts qualify us to be included in this conclave. Agree?"

Scientist agreed, and apologized to Dolphin and the many species of fish and other sea residents who were crammed together in closer waters to get a better look at us. "We haven't ignored you, Dolphin. It's true. Marine biologists have explored just five percent of the oceans' waters. We haven't gathered enough data to fully understand your world yet. As you well know, our task is monumental!"

He paused as if to find the right words. "It's as simple as this, Dolphin. The human species cannot drink saltwater. Being the selfish animal we are, we primarily focus on studying the water resources that are drinkable for us. Less than three percent of the world's waters are freshwaters. This is a serious problem for the animal species that live on land. In many regions of the Earth the availability of drinkable water is so low that millions of life forms are in crisis."

Dolphin interrupted, "Our problems affect you too! The ocean populations are being over-fished to the point where some species are going extinct; and the gross tonnage of toxins you dump into the waters every day seriously affects the viability of the oceans. Certainly impedes the health of your freshwaters and land. You fight your petty wars throughout our habitat, filling it with poisons that will be in the waters for thousands of years. Add in the extent of the United States military testing, and you can see how you are killing us! Can't you find another place to play?" she moaned.

She wasn't finished. "It saddens me to talk about those Dolphins and Orca Whales imprisoned in amusement parks and local aquariums. The aquarium keepers believe they enjoy performing. Some do. There's no other way to get exercise in their confines. Surely the trainers know that their acrobatic 'tricks' are not easy to execute in those small artificial tanks. We often swim one hundred miles a day in open waters. The small tanks holding our cousins just won't do! The dead fish tossed to them as a 'reward' for their 'performances' is humiliating. Their chatter is not because they are happy as so many of you would like to believe. It is their pleas to be free. They haven't lost hope that you'll return them to their home again. I haven't the heart to tell them the truth."

Dolphin's voice quivered. "Just yesterday, my son was captured in waters off the coast of Japan and was placed in a viewing tank. Worldwide television newscasts aired what happened next. He leaped out of the tank to get away, but couldn't make it. His body hung on the railing surrounding his prison. After three attempts to escape, he made it out of the tank area but fell onto the concrete below. He was picked up by his keepers and hustled back to his little tank. Can you imagine his disappointment?" She dove into the Sea as if to clear her head.

In seconds, she emerged to say, "In spite of our ambiguous relationship, we do care about you as we do all life on our planet. Even with the inequity you established between our species, we want you to know our hearts are saddened for the earthquake-tsunami victims in Japan and other coastal regions. No one deserves the kind of suffering the Japanese people are going through these days. Countless residents of the sea and land animals perished along with them. Why didn't you report our losses in your newscasts?"

She nervously swam back and forth in front of us. "You already know that the size of Dolphin and Whale species' cerebral neocortices surpass almost all of the other mammals. Your scientists have yet to quantify the extent of our highly evolved intelligence. We find it interesting that you can't interpret our complex 'speech,'" she clicked. "Try as you may, you cannot master our advanced sonar capability. We are able to locate our favorite food animals and sense dangers miles away by 'hearing' the pulses of their sounds, and in seconds calculate their distance from us by their echoes. Bats have the same ability. You call it 'echolocation.' Unfortunately the military wants to understand our ability so we might spy for them or worse, carry incendiary devices to deliver to their enemies. This is an abomination to our souls!

"We are a peaceful nation. Long before mammals arrived on Earth, the Universe entrusted the Dolphin nation to translate the historical records of the World Soul. When you are ready, we will provide you with information about your true role in the Universe."

We looked at each other. "What is our true role in the Universe?" Healer whispered. Dolphin heard her and smiled as if she were smiling at an innocent child. "When you are able to fully understand Universal knowledge, the collective soul of Humanity will evolve in extraordinary ways. It will be a glorious day for humankind! A fortunate day for the Earth!"

Dolphin effortlessly leaped out of the Sea and dove back to splash water all over those of us standing on the shore. Somehow I don't think it was to make us squeal and laugh.

Scientist looked across the Sea. His face was in anguish. "Everything you said is true, Dolphin! When it comes to people's relationship with the other animals, we are concerned first and foremost with those matters affecting *human* life. People are on top of the food chain. If we must destroy a few species of life forms to satisfy our needs, we will!"

His voice was cracking. "I must be honest with you. We think of the waters of the Earth as home to *our* food supply! Those awful oil spills in the Gulf of Mexico have destroyed the local economy. *Our* economy! Sea Guardians are doing their best to save the sea animal victims impacted by the last spill. But the general public's interest in human loss far outweighs saving the other animals' lives.

"True, humans know little about the water animals, except how delicious they are when well prepared. We are more interested in the animals that live on the Earth as we do. I'm sorry. But that's the way it is."

Scientist's justification of human behavior toward the animals living in the seas sickened Dolphin. She dove deep and would never surface before us again. Scientist would say nothing more, and walked away from us. We watched him disappear in a black fog rising out of the sea.

We made our way back to the clearing without speaking. A new image of Scientist was waiting for us in the circle. Without commenting on what had just happened, she continued the lesson. "Let's get back to the business at hand, shall we?" (I'd forgotten what we were talking about.) Guardian said, "It's going to be hard to concentrate after the disconcerting hours we've just spent with Dolphin." Some were still wiping their eyes.

Impervious to the mood of the group, Scientist continued where her colleague left off. "Prehistoric humans had another advantage over the other animals. With their increased intelligence, they were able to conjure imaginary ways to make their days easier. They came to believe they could better their lives by altering the laws of Nature by using magic and performing rituals to get what they wanted. You might think of their use of their mental advancement over the other animals as a form of 'free will.'"

Teacher interrupted. "That explains how early homo species were able to recognize the difference between the ordinary and the extraordinary. Our ancestors imagined that if they ate an animal or wore its fur, its very nature would become theirs. They thought they would be able to run as fast as the antelope. Be as efficient in the kill as the tiger. At that moment in evolutionary time, humans transcended the mundane and walked out of the bush leaving the animals to fend for themselves. Forever."

Cleric jumped up from his seat shouting, "There's more to 'free will' than an advanced brain part! I don't care how big it is! God gave man free will to choose to believe or choose not to believe in Him. It is the supreme test of faith!"

Televangelist was back! I must admit, I enjoy watching his colorful ways of expressing his "righteousness" almost as much as I disagree with his interpretations of his religion's texts.

Philosopher spoke softly to diffuse Cleric's outburst. "Calm down, Cleric. 'Free will' is a complex philosophical question that has been debated by mystics and religious leaders for centuries. Your religion's belief system is just one way of answering it."

Cleric thought about what Philosopher said for a moment and apologized for his outburst. He did not want to be the cause of dissension in Sanctuary today.

Scientist said, "Look, I'm not challenging those of you who worship a higher power or those of you who subscribe to alternative principles of reality that 'transcend' science. My mind has been opened by all of you, and I intend to keep it open. But I am obligated to say your range of beliefs cannot be possible without the intricacies of our massive cerebral neocortex."

Horse whispered to Fox and Deer who had joined her in the back of the circle. "Here we go again!"

Vigorously scratching behind his ear, Fox said, "Don't they ever get weary of their rhetoric? They can have their 'intellectual' advantage!"

Raven flew from Skeptic's shoulder to a Tree. The Tree stretched one of its branches across the clearing for Raven to perch above us. "And so . . . the era of Humanity took wing. (That's an inside joke)," Raven said. The birds tittered. "I'm not sure your so-called highly evolved brain is the real reason for your extraordinary abilities. There must be another answer we have yet to identify.

"We Ravens know how difficult it was for the early peoples to survive the forces of Nature and us. We listened in on the humans' talking. The people decided that if they spiritually connected with Nature's powerful gods, they would receive protection and food in return. Unfortunately for the animals, 'spiritually connecting' meant 'sacrificing' (slaughtering) millions of us to satisfy the appetites of their gods-goddesses-God. Shamans today continue to believe that animal entrails and bones heal sickness and predict the future," he said.

Raven hopped to a higher branch. "From the beginning of our life together on Earth we have accepted your position on top of the animal hierarchy. If it took dying for the pleasure of your deities, we thought we would be spiritually connected to you somehow."

His feathers rose in disgust. "This is what I don't understand! What thought processes found exclusively in the human brain caused you to believe you must destroy countless of innocent animals for your particular divinity? Furthermore," he shouted to Scientist, "Can you explain to me why the non-human mammals with advanced neocortices have never, EVER sacrificed animals to anyone, let alone to the gods?"

The animals hooted, howled, bellowed, growled, hissed and barked their agreement. Raven flew back to Skeptic's shoulder. Skeptic whispered to Raven, "Good questions, my friend."

Teacher stepped forward clasping and unclasping his hands as if groping the air to find the right words. "We all know how dangerous the human mind is when we are out of control."

Turning to the animals in the clearing, "I'm grateful that you don't hold onto your negative feelings for very long. Dog may get angry with his caretaker for taking his food bowl away, but soon gets over it. No sense in holding onto anger when there are so many other things to do."

Sage looked up. He hadn't spoken in days. "Raven's wisdom is inspiring. I think the meaning of our existence is far more complex than can be explained by religion or science. Maybe the truth about who we are lies beyond the mechanics of our brain or our philosophical beliefs. Science seeks answers somewhere in the physical confines of our bodies to explain how we reason and why we react the way we do toward others. Teachers of most religions expect people to believe (have faith) in an omniscient Divinity who exists somewhere outside of our bodies. I am uncomfortable with both disciplines."

"Think they will ever figure anything out?" Horse asked her companions. Deer shook her head. She was busy licking the salt off of Horse's sweaty leg. (Horse had enjoyed a marvelous gallop before the meeting.)

Fox mumbled, "Humans are so busy complicating the cause of our existence that it's a wonder they get anything done!"

Sage heard Fox and chuckled. "You're so right, Fox. We humans complicate everything we do and spend most of our time talking about it. We lose the intention of our questions because we distract ourselves by discussing the alternatives ad infinitum. And now I'm going to propose another alternative that might shed some light on the animals' question. Be patient with me?" The animals trusted Sage over and above all the other Universal Images, and quieted down.

Sage's eyes flashed brightly. It was hard to look into them. He walked the perimeter of the clearing until he stopped in front of Scientist. "There can be no 'effect' without a 'cause.' This is a basic law of physics. Am I right, Scientist?" Scientist nodded. "Well then, I suggest we do not go further in our quest until we take a hard look at our Universe's beginnings. There is so much more to reveal about our origins that either Religionists or Scientists can figure out."

Sage sat down in a chair made of woven branches that had

appeared in the center of the circle. The elder leaned forward, elbows on his knees. His hands hung loosely between his legs. "Religions teach a 'Creator' caused the Universe to appear out of 'nothing,' and now rules his-her creation for eternity. Scientists will have 'nothing' to do with the idea of a 'creator.' They think they have a better answer."

Sage stopped mid-sentence and looked down at his feet. A tiny fox kit was attempting to climb up his leg. He gently picked the baby up and put her in his lap. Continuing, "Some scientists suggest that the energy of the heat generated by the Big Bang created a 'googleplex' of sub-atomic particles without a known purpose other than knocking into each other until the heat cooled down. After some 350 million years when the Universe did cool down, it is believed that the particles adhered to each other to become the first building blocks of matter -- atoms. It took billions more years for first matter to become all matter in our Universe."

Sage cleared his throat. The sound startled the baby fox who jumped off her perch, and scooted under Sage's chair. "What fascinates me most is that mainstream Science's brightest minds continue to ignore the first and most logical question, 'What caused the 'Big Bang?'

"Why do mainstream scientists avoid the question? Do they fear that if they found the cause of the Big Bang it would prove a 'creator' exists? Can't they see how incomplete their assumptions are?" Scientist squirmed. She was not pleased with Sage disputing centuries of scientific research. As if patting Scientist on the head he looked at her and said, "Bear with me a moment, will you?" Clearly agitated, Scientist stared straight ahead, hands folded.

Sage stood and began to pace. "I agree with the theory that our Universe rose out of a singular source – possibly the first atom. I disagree with those who deny the idea that 'something' existed before the seed-atom. Why not consider the possibility that a super-intelligent energy field existed long before the Universe began to expand?"

The elder was excited by his idea. "The energy field produced matter within itself. As itself. The intrinsic nature of both energy and matter was as one body. The extraordinary power of their adjoining is the actual cause of the Big Bang. This would be the grandest 'effect' of all time! Together, never to separate, Energy and Matter became an infinite singularity . . . all that is the Universe."

Sage paused as if he remembered we were still listening to him. Then said, "Have I confused you?" Scientist wasn't confused. Smiling for the first time, she said, "You make sense, Sage! Theoretical physicists believe the particles that comprised the primordial atom still exist today. From the moment of their mergence, energy and matter have transformed from one state to another. It is probable that the water we drink right here in Sanctuary and on Earth has existed in countless forms from the beginning. However, I dispute your theory that water is conscious of its existence. It is impossible to validate . . . pure conjecture."

Undaunted, Sage continued, "Why not go further with this idea? Can we be neither created not destroyed? Could our (yours and my) energy-matter bodies have transformed from one state to another from the very moment of the Big Bang?"

Scientist said, "I have to think it. I'll get back to you on that."

"They are beginning to see Nature as we do," Dog whispered into Cat's ear. Cat was busy cleaning Dog's face. "Dog, you need a bath," he whispered back.

"Many new physicists are taking the path of the Mystics whether they acknowledge it or not." Sage said. "Since ancient times, Mystics profess that all that is seen and unseen is one state of 'being.' Long ago, they named this state of being 'Consciousness.' Now it's Science's turn to open up to the possibility. May I explain?" There was no doubt Sage had our attention.

"Consciousness cannot be detected, defined, identified, or explained through purely scientific means. Mystics believe Consciousness is the undetectable coalescence forming and linking all matter and energy. It is the causal factor that creates life. Consciousness is the animating principle unifying what appears to be physically separate such as humans from animals, trees from rocks, water from air and so forth."

After a long moment, Sage spoke slowly. "There is much more. Consciousness is the force of attraction between particles of matter and between quantities of energy that we call gravity. Consciousness activates the energy for plants to grow and causes the rivers to flow into the sea. It is the plants, the rivers, and the sea. Consciousness is the dark space between the celestial bodies in our cosmos. It is the celestial bodies.

"Consciousness activates the atoms to form cells within our bodies. It is the space inside the atoms forming the cells. It is the electrical energy in our brains stimulating our very thoughts. It is the electromagnetic force responsible for every phenomenon we encounter in daily life. If we personify Consciousness, it is our life force, our spirit, our soul, the air we breathe. It is our breath."

Sage took a breath and looked around the circle with profound love emanating from his whole being. I basked in it. "In this context, we are Consciousness. We must recognize within our deepest spiritual selves that we are interconnected to all that exists."

Wind stopped to listen. Sanctuary was listening. Consciousness itself was listening.

The colors of the celestial bodies illuminated the clearing in agreement with what Sage was saying. "Yes, dear ones," Sage said. "Humans have an evolved cerebral cortex, but please consider this. Consciousness, as conscious energy, existed long before there were bodies, let alone brains."

The group looked around the circle at each other as if taking a silent poll. Several turned to talk to each other. Clearly, some disagreed with Sage's theory. After considering the alternatives, the consensus was Sage's view could be possible.

Sage's body began to glow brighter and brighter. I tried to cover my eyes but there would be no looking away. The intense light that once was Sage filled me. Where were the other animals, the forest, and the people? I heard frantic calls from the others who too were blinded by the light. Someone grabbed my hand. Cat pressed against me.

A voice emitted from the light saying, "Don't be afraid! I am appearing to you as my true Self." Sage's voice seemed to come from everywhere. It echoed through our bodies, brought us to our knees. "Surely you know that my Self is your Self. Our connection is as real as every being we see or can't see. We are in dynamic relationship with all that exists. We are the undetectable coalescence connecting matter and energy. When our body no longer functions in its present form, we continue to exist as we always have existed. Undetected, undefined, unidentified, unexplained."

Gradually, the light faded. We were able to see each other once more. I recognized the shapes of individual forms. I couldn't help but think, "It's easy to forget I am all that is when I see the others in separate bodies."

Sage's voice echoed across the clearing. "Just as you are thinking, Q, it is easy to forget who we are. It's easy to disown your true Self in the 'reality' of our three-dimensional world where you see every thing and every one separate from you. Realize this. Your true Self is One Being, being One.

"Until we fully accept our membership within one dynamic system, the other animals and Earth's natural resources remain disconnected from us. In reality, it is impossible for us to separate from the other animals! For that matter, impossible for us to separate from all that is in the Universe! *This* is the answer to the animals' question. This, dear friends, is the message we must take back to our beloved Earth. We must."

Silence. We were alone. We tried to reacquaint ourselves with our surroundings without Sage's presence.

Change Maker broke the silence. "What just happened? I think that somewhere along the line people lost confidence in their own instincts and allowed others to do their thinking, even choose their beliefs for them. When that happened, we disconnected from each other."

Communicator changed her seat to be next to Skeptic. "Skeptic, I've spent much time thinking about our behavior toward each other that awful day we destroyed Sanctuary. Drifting alone in my bubble through the abyss I battled with my ego over the anger that I'd bottled up. I must admit I was furious with people who didn't properly care for the other animals. Your 'scientific-philosophical' views about animal experimentation became the center of my fury. Can you forgive me?" Skeptic covered her hands with his.

Philosopher was moved. "Communicator, Skeptic, you couldn't resolve your differences. How could you? Our beliefs are formed by our individual experiences. Communicator, it has been your experience that animals 'talk' to people and are able to communicate with their own species as well as other species. Skeptic, by using 'scientific procedures," you embellished the Church's creation story; thus strengthening man's position of 'dominion over the animals' by 'proving' that animals are soulless. Unfortunately, your pronouncements continue to influence worldwide beliefs and attitudes about them." Skeptic looked miserable. He was deeply sorry he caused so much harm to the animals. Raven nuzzled his head into Skeptic's hand to comfort him.

The circle closed in. Knee to knee, butt to butt, hands holding paws, nuzzling and hugging, we pressed against each other. We didn't want to lose each other again. The birds and other tree creatures sitting above us in the canopy giggled at the sight of us scrunching together. Actually, the tree dwellers were huddled together as much as possible too. Monkey jumped from a low-hanging vine onto my shoulder. His little hands tightly held onto my hair. I didn't care. It felt good to me. Our physical bodies separated us, but in this moment we became the One Being we have always been.

Secret was watching us and happily whispered. "You know! You *really* know!" Humanity was sitting just below the branch where Secret was sitting. She looked at Secret lovingly and smiled for the first time since she arrived. Humanity's voices sang in its monotone chorus,

"It's all so simple. We are perfect. Perfect as every moment. Not one virus, bacteria, flood, fire, earthquake . . . Not one garbage dump, polluted river, ghetto, scream, slap, cancer is out of place.

"We are all that is. Slime trapped in the corner of a pristine pool holding broken Styrofoam cups, beer cans, chicken bones. Perfectly placed. On this day at this hour, we are Dog chained tightly in the sun . . . water bowl empty. We are Cat left outside in the freezing cold . . . We are Chicken force-fed and crammed in enclosure never to see the sun her entire lifetime. We are Horse whipped across the finish line . . . meat if we can't show."

Humanity's awful words disturbed me to my very core. I looked at the others' faces hoping I wasn't alone with my reaction. I was disappointed to see they were nodding in agreement with her. How could they agree with what Humanity was saying? I held my ears, but couldn't block out what was said next.

"We are Elephant forced to tear down her own rain forest. She must beg for her own food at night in the squalid cities of Thailand, then return hungry to work long hours the next day. We are street Bear in Turkey with a spike driven through our snout to control us as we perform tricks for passers-by."

Humanity lowered her head. We had to strain to hear the chorus.

"I'm so tired of the battle. Me in combat with me. Me manifesting dis-ease, dis-order, chaos. Me torturing innocent ones. Me afraid of my secrets. Me always hiding from me."

The Universal Image of Humanity knotted what was left of a tattered golden cord tightly around her waist and looked across the circle, hoping someone else might speak. She reached down to scratch Goose's head. Ferret hesitated, then moved in for a nuzzle. Both dashed out of the way when Humanity jumped up.

First sobbing, then laughing, *"Get it? I get it! Then I lose it. I spiral the spiral dizzy with the beauty as well as the chaos. I am exhilarated by the splendor of the Being that embraces – is – who I am.*

Can't you see? It's all so simple!"

THIRTEEN
That they come into their own

For a moment I tolerated what Humanity was saying, although I despised the images she evoked. Not able to bear anymore, I wailed, "I most certainly can separate me from the things I don't want to be part of. I am not the slime in a pool! I am not Dog chained in the hot sun! I am the same person I was when I arrived in Sanctuary.

A gentle voice asked, "What's wrong with you, Q? Are you trying to ignore what you've discovered?"

Without looking for the source of the voice, I whispered, "No. I don't understand any of it, that's all."

My inner voice interrupted, "What are you doing? Can't you remember why we came to Sanctuary in the first place? The animals' question is about why they were separated from humanity at the spiritual level. It's not about slime in a pool. What does that mean?"

A cloud of rainbow colors whirled into the circle. The group was delighted. I felt disoriented. Couldn't think. Where am I?

Cat rubbed against my leg. "Hey!" he me-owed. "Stay with us!"

A gentle breeze caressed my face. Not even Sanctuary could distract me from what I dread to face back on Earth. I shouted angrily to everyone within earshot, "What about the destruction? Have you forgotten the wars, child abuse, animals starving and neglected, the ecological devastation? Who is responsible for all this?" I looked into every face in the circle. All I could see was their shock at my rage. Before anyone could answer my question I answered it. "We are! Humanity, how can you say, 'everything is perfect in the moment?"

"Why do you only remember the suffering?" the voices of Humanity asked.

"Why can't *you* remember, Humanity? I can't forget any of it!" Tears welling up, my very life force was weakening. Not now! I came here as the leader of this expedition. I was the motivator. Always the optimist.

I covered my face with my hands. Didn't want the others to see me cry. Oh no! My tears are driving the other animals away. They're leaving the circle and walking toward the horizon. I pleaded, "Don't go! Don't leave me!"

The Universal Images stood up and hurriedly walked out of the circle to catch up with the animals. The crowd disappeared except for Humanity who stood next to me. I reached out to touch her. Shaking her head, she abruptly turned her back and walked away. She had lost interest. Why can't I get it? Somewhere deep inside of me I know the truth. All I have to do is get out of my own way to remember it.

Humanity is almost out of sight. Somehow I know the small speck I see is not who I think it is. It's me! Of course! I am Humanity! I am walking away from me! That can't be! I'm right here. All I have to do is take one step. Change my mind. Surrender to my true Self.

Surrender? I don't know how. I have been taught that "surrendering," means giving up, letting go and abstaining, losing control. Surrendering is weakness, loss, lying down before the enemy. Who made up this nonsense? Surrendering is impossible. If I do exist as some sort of cosmic Consciousness, then I am all that is. Right? So why can't I change the rules? Why can't I have it all?

My detractor (me) stepped in again and said, "Listen! All that has happened here in Sanctuary has been some sort of a dream. An illusion you created. The animals, the people, even Sanctuary were figments of our imagination!"

"No, you are wrong!" I say to myself. "This place, the people, the other animals were as real as I am (if I am real)." I fell to my knees and put my face in the ground. I was glad everyone had gone. My muffled cries into the dirt mixed with my tears would have made them wonder if I'd gone mad. Maybe I have. Is it madness to know that when I hurt others, I hurt me? When I laugh at others, I am laughing at me? When I cry for others, I am crying for me? If this is madness, I've arrived.

Sanctuary's splendorous landscape became two-dimensional. Its trees and flowers appeared to be copies of Nature that were made by not very skillful artists. Where is everybody? Must I stay here alone? I'm not here (or there) or anywhere. How can I live without the others?

I don't know how it happened but it did. Maybe it was because I was too tired to argue with me anymore. Warm, sweet energy filled me with what can only be described as how I feel when I've fallen in love. When I am in love, I unconditionally accept the one I love. I consciously surrender my body, mind and spirit to my beloved. When I am in love, the world becomes magical. I savor every bite I take and every flower I smell. Being in love puts everything else on hold.

A newly expanded feeling resembling "being in love" filled me over and above the deepest love I've ever felt for another. There is no single "other" to love. This feeling is conscious of itself as itself. This love is vast, glorious, absolute. It is boundless, luminescent, and eternal. This state of "being in love" rushes through my body and overwhelms my spirit. I am able to surrender to who I am. It's so simple!

∞

I KNOW IN MY INNERMOST BEING that no one or thing is outside my Self. I am (we are) all of it. We are the seen and the unseen, and live in the multiple dimensions of time and space. We populate the Universe as One being. We are the unseen deva, drala, kami, nature spirits, avatars, the angels.

A warm mist moistened my face. I lay down on sweet smelling grasses, and looked up into the skies. The phenomenon reminded me of the northern polar lights of the Aurora Borealis over the Alaskan Arctic. The Cree Indian people call it the "Dance of the Spirits." Here in Sanctuary the colors are otherworldly, the lights more spectacular. Has this newly awakened consciousness of my Consciousness revealed itself as an incredible show in the sky?

"You *are* mad!" I say to me. "How can you surrender when

the others won't surrender along with you? If you surrender and the others don't, what happens then? Why should you be the only one surrendering today? It's not fair!" I sat up and looked around me. I had the sensation that Sanctuary was waiting for me to respond.

I recalled a koan that American Buddhist teacher and author, Robert Thurman interpreted at a conference on "Buddhism in America" in Estes Park, Colorado.

"Proposition Number One. *The world – this world – is a horrible place! I mean that! Horrible! Africa and AIDS. Millions of AIDS orphans . . . the wars . . . the violence . . . the prisons . . . our own inner cities . . . family brutality even in the middle class . . . I mean this world is really a horrible place! The loss of other species! The destruction of life and the habitat, and so forth . . . Anyone living in denial of all that is kind of kidding himself or herself . . . That is Proposition Number One.*

"Proposition Number Two. *(which can be understood on many different levels) is that this world is an exquisitely beautiful place . . . I don't know if you walked outside after the afternoon workshops. Before the sun went down, if you looked at the feathery clouds above the valley, the way they were touched and tinged with golden light, the way the high altitude wind currents made them fluff and puff into kind of little Buddha lands . . . It was enough to completely make you pass out if you looked at them carefully . . . Yes, the world is a totally horrible place and it's a magnificently beautiful place. That is Proposition Number Two.*

"Proposition Number Three. *One who is enlightened does not move callously from the horror to the beauty and park itself there . . . and doesn't leave the suffering in this terrible veil of woe and hang out in the blissful paradises . . . among the fringes of the clouds. As a wise Japanese philosopher's wonderful metaphor: 'Both are in a condition of double exposure like a doubly exposed negative of awareness.' Both are instantaneously and simultaneously perceived. Not seeing*

*the total horror and total beauty simultaneously . . . would
be the supreme tolerance of cognitive dissonance. And that is
Proposition Number Three."*

MAYBE IT WAS GRACE or maybe it was remembering most of the koan
or maybe I just stopped thinking. A star exploded lighting up
the cosmos. In an instant I could understand how both darkness
and light exist together as one moment. It has been my refusal to
recognize the cognitive dissonance separating me from the others
and everything else that is.

Sitting on the soft ground in Sanctuary I am more alive
than I have ever felt before. Now I understand why I am that
slime floating on that pristine pool *and* I am the pure water
of the pool holding the slime. Everything is in its place. By
consciously becoming One Being, my ego and my true Self exist
simultaneously. It is so simple! The "yeah buts" that flow into my
head every time I am confused and armed for a debate are gone.

In this very moment, I realize I am safe wherever I am. Even
in the darkness of the unknown. After all, I *am* the unknown. I
am all of Existence. There is no "other." No "someone!" I am that
"other." I am that "someone." This is the message that has been
repeated over and over by Mystics down through the ages. No
matter how often I've heard it, I had to get there by my self. My
Self.

Without giving me a chance to think about it, I interrupted
me for what would be the last time. "How can you be the song of a
bird when you know a cat nearby is planning to end the melody?
How can you be so arrogant that you would willingly accept the
cat's plan to kill that bird when you can chase him away? Maybe
save the bird's life? What is your responsibility to the bird and the
cat if you stop controlling the outcomes? Who in hell (or heaven)
do you think you are?"

THERE WOULD BE NO MORE DEBATE. The battle within waged without
me. After a while, my dark thoughts faded and I fell asleep. I
became Raven soaring across the meadows. From my height
in the sky I saw Squirrel searching the ground for food for her
kittens safely ensconced in their tree nest. I saw Wolf watching
Squirrel, waiting for her to move a bit further away from the tree.

Hunter was on a hill aiming at Wolf. All were interconnected in one single moment. All doing what they know how to do. They are what they do. I finally understood what was happening. It doesn't matter that Hunter missed, or Wolf couldn't grab her meal-to-go when Squirrel escaped up the tree, or her kittens still had their quick mother around to feed them. There would be another time, another day.

The animals exist in simultaneous beauty and horror all their lives. Tolerate cognitive dissonance? They don't know what that means. I'm not sure I know what it means. The animals don't have to be taught who they are. They are what they are. There is no discussion. The animals don't have to surrender to their own nature. They are their own nature. Being human, I have to think about it. Be taught who I am.

We humans have been blessed and cursed with the ability to debate our own questions. We demand unconditional faith in our religions' texts, as well as in our scientific views. We are too busy trying to prove our myths. Maybe the "Tree of Knowledge" found in mythologies all over the world bore the fruits of Knowing. "Knowledge" and "Knowing" are two separate concepts. Awesome concepts, but worlds apart. If the mythological Tree of Knowledge bore fruits of Knowing, I am drawn to the idea that Eve's reputation was sacrificed for her knowing the Truth. Perhaps first Woman knew (if only briefly) she was a conscious being dwelling among conscious life forms in a conscious Universe. She excitedly shared the knowledge with her alter ego, first Man. As they talked over the meaning of her discovery, they became confused. Then were afraid. Their doubts separated them from each other and the understanding of who they were. With that, Eden was lost.

I can't believe that Consciousness would banish Itself from Eden for trying to understand Its Self. It makes a great story though considering billions of people believe (have faith) in the mythological versions. Belief and faith are such weak descriptions when we try to figure out that which we cannot understand. We rely on our heroes to explain to us who we are and how we fit into our world. For that matter, how we fit into our everyday lives.

LIGHT SLOWLY RETURNED TO SANCTUARY and cleared the fog. I've been looking for the answers in the wrong places. I now know I can lovingly serve those who can't surrender to their Universal connection with all that is (yet). My bliss will become everyone's bliss. My peace will become everyone's peace. In this very moment I now understand what the heroic Universal Images of great people realized just hours ago. What took me so long?

There isn't a question left in my head. I wish I understood what just happened. I'll have to think about it. "No!" I say gently to me. "Stop right there! Thinking about it is what brought us here in the first place! "

I looked up to see my companions leaving Sanctuary. They have become what they have always been. Light Beings, they are moving on – fading, melting, misting, rising. I ran toward them shouting, "Wait for me! Where are you going? Wait for me! Wait! Wait!" Someone grabbed my hand, and I was lifted up into the air with the others. Hand in hand, paw-to-paw, wing-to-wing, fin-to-fin, buzz-to-buzz, we effortlessly rose into the skies beyond Sanctuary and onward into the darkness of outer space. I looked back for a moment, but could leave Sanctuary without regrets. After all, I am Sanctuary and can return to me whenever I want to. Sanctuary exists everywhere. No matter where we go and no matter who we are, we are there.

What the . . .? We are returning to the third dimension! I'm not sure I can bear the limitations of "reality" we endured in our three dimensional world. I hope I will always remember our adventure in the "true" reality of multiple dimensions.

Without remorse, the Universal Images are releasing the personas that defined them. Separated from their Universal Image, the individual personalities are returning to the times from which they came as fast as they can. Into their time. Into my time. Only this time we are returning consciously as One Thought, One Being. Will we alter history as we remember it? What have we accomplished? Will we ever, ever know? We soared across the cosmos confidently chanting our chants, chirping, screeching, barking, roaring, hissing, clicking.

As we soared away from Sanctuary, someone wondered, "What about the animals living on other planets? Is there a hierarchy of life forms in a galaxy far, far away where a few on top of their system are causing dissonance and separation from the others? Should we go there and find out?"

Oh no! Here we go again!

Wait! I hear them! Across the distances of space, I hear children's voices calling, pleading, *"Chaco, Chaaco, Chaacoo! Where are you? Please come home. Chaco . . . Chaco! Are you sleeping, Chaco? Wake up Chaco!"* Curiosity got the better of me and in an instant I was back in Sanctuary. The others waved goodbye, and continued on their way. I watched their light streaks fade as they shot into deep space. They no longer need a light path to return to the source of our beginning. After all, *we* are the source of our beginning.

My skin is tingling! The hairs on my arm are standing on end. I am covered with goose bumps. Change tickles. My legs are throbbing as the transformation continues. My muscles are growing firm and hard. My body is filled with a power I never felt as human. New coarse hair grows and covers me. I am a golden color! My fingers have shortened and withdrawn into my palms. My palms have become black pads. Claws move out from within the pads. Pads? Claws? Paws? I have paws! I can run now. Faster than fast now. I bet I can run forever!

The voices are getting louder, more urgent. *"Chaco! Chaaco!"* One of them is crying, *"Where are you? Please come back, Chaco. We miss you so much. I love you Chaco!"* My arms have become legs. I have four legs! As soon as I realized this, I dropped to the ground on all fours. My balance is much better. My face! My face is gone! How can anyone recognize me with so much fur? My snout has grown longer. My nose is black. All I know is I like this new look.

I sat down on my haunches and scratched behind my ears. Feels good. My hearing and sense of smell have increased many-fold and I am not confused by it. Unbelievable! I can discern the sounds and smells of each and every animal and plant in Sanctuary. The water rush is singing. The water's taste is fresher than any fresh I've ever tasted. In human form, scents and sounds blur together. My new senses are fun! I even hear the sound of the bats' wings soaring in that fabulous cave I fell into so long ago. The bats know they are transformed by my transformation. What took me so long to realize who I am? They knew who I was all along. Why didn't I?

"Chaco! Do you hear me? Chaco! Where are you?" An adult

human voice demands, "Chaco! Where are you, Chaco! We love you, Chaco, but you make me mad sometimes. Come home now!"

I can't wait to get back to my family. My Cat friend Bhapu jumped onto my back to hitch a ride. We turned to look at the sacred clearing in Sanctuary where we gathered so many times. I am filled with gratitude to the Universe for sharing itself with me. My love has grown beyond the love ever felt by anyone, anywhere, any time, every time, in all time.

The Curtains Close.

A stagehand re-opened them. We have lined up across the stage for our bow. We are professional actors so we keep smiling even though we are dismayed at the empty theater. The floors are covered with playbills and paper cups. When did the audience walk out? Did the people leave when I changed into a magnificent collie? How could they not be impressed with my acting? Didn't they get it? Someone is out there in the dark. Clapping hands echo across the giant room. At least one member of the audience enjoyed the play. I wonder who that person is. I try to see a face in the shadows. Another illusion? Maybe that person is the shadow.

Outside the Theater.

The audience emerged from the theater, and as quickly as they had become one body, they broke away from each other and became individual personalities again. Some were crying, some angry, few were laughing.

"That play was ridiculous! I never witnessed anything so preposterous in my life! Animals have souls? Then, I have three legs!"

"I'm going home and let my dog and cat come into the house tonight."

"It was hard to face harsh animal situations that I've always ignored. I want to help the animals, but how?"

"Sympathy for the animals' plight? Not as long as there is fast cheap food available at McDonald's and Burger King. I will draw the line at eating veal, though."

"We are One Being being One? I think I get it! But how can I explain it?"

"Impossible! You can't change human behavior. We own the

Earth, and that's that!"

"I didn't understand any of it."

"Must say the special effects fascinated me. I love the idea of a place called Sanctuary!"

"Bizarre! Read the critic's review before you buy our next theater tickets, OK? I came here tonight to be entertained. Not to be criticized for being human."

Diana and I are the last ones in the theater. Still sitting frozen in our seats, we whispered to each other, "What just happened?" She said, "Q, I can't make sense out of my humanity. The play was about an incompletely evolved species which I am a member of. Will we ever step outside of ourselves?"

I had no answer but wanted to talk about it further. "I need a cup of coffee! Want to join me?"

She declined. "Not this time, Q. I have to think about what happened. Can we talk later?" Her friends pulled up to the curb in their old station wagon and asked me if I wanted a ride.

I thanked them and said, "I need to clear my head. Besides, I have friends waiting for me."

As I walked, I reached into my pocket and found the stone! *The* Stone! I thought I'd lost it! Now it's back! It has changed from simply blue into sparkling unworldly colors, and is still warm to the touch. Holding it in my hand reminded me of my adventure in that crystalline cave with those marvelous bats. An Indian friend once told me that the Indian nations believe stones are "people" just as the animals and plants are. Every Stone is an ancient being who knows every story about life on our Earth and probably about life in the Universe. After all, the "Stone People" originated from the same source of our creation as we did.

The Stone People arrived on Earth as celestial bodies. They crashed onto our planet and sculpted its formations. They rose out of the volcanoes to become the mountains. They rise above us as cliffs, and massage our toes as grains of sand. They were re-arranged to form a circle forty-six hundred years ago on Salisbury Plain in England. Built by ancient Britons who left no written record, Stonehenge continuously inspires questions about why they were assembled. Most historians assume it was a place of spiritual ritual.

Countless Stone People have been sculpted into deities to be revered. The idea of being alive has been a mystery to us since we began thinking about it. Stone images of gods and goddesses of ancient India, Egypt, Greece and Asian civilizations symbolize people's quest for spiritual purpose. Some of the most artistically perfect carvings can be found throughout Europe in places of worship.

Two thousand miles off the coast of Chile in the middle of a vast ocean is a small island named Rapa Nui, also called Easter Island. Hundreds of giant carvings of unknown, remarkably similar forms can be found all over the island. Carved from volcanic rock a thousand years ago, there is no written record about what or who they were. The people living on the island proudly protect the sculptures carved and installed by their ancestors. Anthropologists believe they portray powerful beings standing watch over the barren land. Perhaps to remind us of the consequences when humans interfere (consume) their abundant environment.

Stone People become priceless when placed in a ring setting and presented to someone with love, and the love is returned. I must never forget that. I won't. I will remember everything that happened. I must.

Last Word.

She's coming! I can't see her, but it's her all right! I'd know the sound of her heels anywhere. My tail is practically wagging off my rear. We've been waiting for her. She left a bowl of water and some biscuits for us. Before she turned the corner, I knocked the bowl over. Didn't matter. The biscuits were delicious.

There she is! She bent down to stroke my head. I stretched and stood up to nudge my snout into her hands. Then she did something she rarely does. She got down on her knees and hugged my neck. I dropped to the ground. Scratch my belly, please? Clipping my leash back onto my collar, she reconnected herself to me. We're a team, my friend and I.

"Come, Chaco! Where's Bhapu?" she said. Cat jumped out of a bush where he'd been napping and rubbed against her leg. She picked him up and hugged him then gently put him down. "It's been a long evening. Guess my play needs some revision. I must say, you both were magnificent, though. How did you two get back here ahead of me?" Together, side-by-side, we walked home. Bhapu ran ahead of us, turning back every few steps to make sure we were coming. We were.

The End.

Epilogue
(Maybe . . .)

*W*HY AM I DRIVEN *to find a spiritual connection with the animals?* Maybe I should move into a windy, freezing cave high on a Tibetan mountaintop as so many monks and yogis have done for thousands of years to get the answers. Should I sacrifice my comfort and eat nothing but nettles, let my hair and skin turn green because of my sparse diet and allow my clothing to rot off before I wake up to realize my place in the Universe? What will it take to get on with it?

Have I learned anything? I continue to wish for retribution upon the horse beaters for causing so much fear and pain upon their innocent victims. Here's the awful truth. Maybe it doesn't work that way. Perhaps the pain and anger I feel is some sort of karmic recompense because I was cruel to horses in another lifetime. Whether karmic law exists or not, I am no better or worse than the others. It depends on who believes what is right and what is not right.

I'd rather be a Mountain. As Mountain, I'd embrace the great greatness I am. I'd be the spirit of the Mountain and rise into the skies ten times beyond my Mountain height. I'd be all that is a Mountain. My forests, waterways, and the animals living on and in me. I'd be tickled by the Earthworms moving my soil. I am wondrous! I'd give myself a great big giant Mountain hug if I could.

Maybe the myths about God and Consciousness and karma and life after death are impossibilities we invented somewhere along the way to comfort ourselves whenever we sink into our fears of the unknown. Maybe our belief systems and related laws don't apply to the laws of the Universe. Do we know the laws of the Universe? Maybe we've missed the truth about the meaning of existence by a long shot, and the ponderings of philosophers and scientists are mind games we play. Maybe the poet in us is trying to calm our collective soul. That's all.

Maybe the imaginings of esoteric possibilities are aberrant, unexplainable activity of the brain and our dreams are nothing but brain waves clearing out the day's activities in disorganized images. Maybe it is arrogance to believe we have soul-energy that never ceases to exist. Maybe we live because of the simple physical process of germination and we are a biological phenomenon that is living by chance. Maybe, when our body is dead, our brain is dead, our life force is dead and we're dead. It's over. We are over. There is nothing more to it.

Maybe intelligent life forms living on other worlds like ours are seeking their own spiritual truths. Perhaps civilizations in a galaxy far, far away are tinkering with the same manifestations of their imaginations too. Or could it be our beliefs are minor notes that can't fit into a cosmic symphony that is being performed somewhere out in the celestials by advanced beings who have no intention of allowing our primitive species to hear (let alone know) the whole score? Maybe we've been using the switch on ourselves and someday we'll fall on the wayside without ever knowing who we truly are.

Q.

Acknowledgments

Countless people have shaped worldviews about the animals. In this tale, ten heroic characters, so-called "Universal Images" represented them. The heroes traveled to an incredible otherworld called Sanctuary to engage in a point/counterpoint discussion about the animals' **QUESTION**. They soon learned that the adventure they embarked on would be far more exciting than just talking about the issues.

Some of the heroic Universal Images resemble people out of past history whose ambiguous scientific perspectives and unique philosophies laid the foundation for worldwide perceptions about what is and what isn't true about animals. Their names may ring a bell, perhaps are answers to a college quiz. Names that pass into the night as soon as the tests are over.

Aristotle	First to classify animal souls into a hierarchal system.
Annie Besant	Man's cruelty to animals proves there is no God.
Edgar Cayce	Trans-psychic; telepathic-clairvoyant.
Charles Darwin	Evolution proves that "man is an animal."
Rene Descartes	"I think, therefore I am. Animals are machines..."
Carl Jung	Inspired the formation of the "Universal Images."
Rudolph Steiner	"All this, comprised in one, art thou!"
Thomas of Aquinas	"God isn't interested in the animals."

Several widely respected people shared their views with the author in interviews. Their work, writings and ideas became the building blocks of the story. They provide balance to the beliefs and attitudes about the other animals that originated out of the past. Listed are a few among many other renowned people who inspired the characterizations of the Universal Images.

·David Bale	(1941 - 2003) Director of non-profits protecting animals worldwide.
Dr. Neil Barnard	Physician's Committee Responsible Medicine.
Deepak Chopra	"A single reality embraces all worlds, times... "
·Gail Eisnitz	Humane Farming Association; food animal guardian.
Matthew Fox	*Sheer Joy: Conversations with Thomas Aquinas.*
Gangaji	"I am, therefore I think."
Jane Goodall	Jane Goodall Institute; *50 Years at Gombe*; Chimpanzee research; Roots & Shoots youth prog.
·Temple Grandin	*Thinking in Pictures: My Life with Autism* — courage, and creativity helping food animals.
·J. Regina Hyland	Author, minister; *Humane Religion*, Journal; *God's Covenant with Animals*.(NY, Lantern Books, 2000)

Samantha Khury	Animal Communicator; Interspecies Comm.
•**"Keeper;"**	Zoo curator/director. Who are zoos for?
•**Joyce Leake**	Animal Communicator; Animal University.
•**Joanne Lauck Hobbs**	*The Voice of the Infinite in the Small;* Educator.
•**Dorothy Maclean**	*To Hear the Angels Sing;*
	Voices of nature spirits. Co-Founder of the Findhorn Community.
Ingrid Newkirk	People for the Ethical Treatment of Animals
•**Lynda Nuttall**	Cheyenne River Sioux; Native Amer. perspective.
•**Priest, Rabbi, Minister, Nun**	Perspectives from their Religion's conscience.
•**Lewis Regenstein**	Author: *Replenish the Earth; The Politics of Extinction;America the Poisoned.*
Jane Roberts/ Rob Butts/Seth	"Animals' ... lives spell out life's meaning."
•**Michael J Roads**	*Talking With Nature/Journey Into Nature;* author and spiritual teacher.
•**Penelope Smith**	Communicator; *Animal Talk; Species Link: Journal of Interspecies Communication*
•**Rupert Sheldrake**	*Dogs That Know When Their Owners Come Home;* Proponent Morphic Biologist, Author
•**Gloria Steinem**	Feminist; humanitarian; change maker.
•**Linda Tellington-Jones**	*The Tellington TTouch;* animal healer
Robert Thurman	Buddhist priest, teacher. "...a tolerance for cognitive dissonance..."
•**Eryn Wolfwalker**	Teacher/practitioner animal healing modalities; natural Farrier

Without whom, this story would never have been told:

Jim Anaston-Karas	Mary Ann Bergfeld
Iva Blacker	Nancy Bureau
Regina Cruz	Evelyn Dickman
Mike Dickmann	Connie Ekrem
Tim Fitzwater	Evangeline Ford
Laura Ford	Martha Gibb
Georgeann Harding	Deborah Hellman
Bruce Hensel	Nancy Hensel
Terri Jacobson	Dorothy Jensen
Peter Jones	Angela Just
Nancy Karas	Samantha Khury
Judy Langberg	Sandra Lovett
CJ McCarthy	Vidya McClutchey
Beth Avila McCracken	Jennifer Ruiz
Rhoda Pollack Cheroutes	Cathleen Simpson
Linda Taylor	Ann Tinkham
Emelia Welber	Jack Welber
Phillip Welber	Jo Lynne Whiting
Eryn Wolfwalker	Barbara Wood

ABOUT THE AUTHOR

After spending several years in Public Relations initiating and organizing award-winning multi-state community relations projects on behalf of a global telecommunications company, Judith Hensel has written her first fictional book, *THE QUESTION "What Happened to the Animal-Human Spiritual Connection?"*

The book is a fantasy about characters created out of real life people who join the animals in an imaginary setting to find the answer to their question. Among articles published about the book's premises, one article "Animals and Humans: Evolving Together in a Conscious Universe," was published in *QUEST* magazine, a publication of the Theosophical Society in America, and inspired the magazine's content theme.

As a former Associate Professor of Art and Humanities, St. Xavier University, Chicago, she received numerous awards as an artist and teacher including special recognition by the Associated Press and the Governor of Illinois. She wrote and directed two critically acclaimed rock operas, *"Hosanna!"* and *"Taproot"* performed by student talent as well as talent from across the Chicago region to sell-out audiences. Her artwork is in several private collections in Australia, the Netherlands, New York, Illinois, California, Colorado and Wisconsin; and for several years was available at the Art Institute of Chicago rental gallery. She holds the MSA in Painting and Graphics, University of Wisconsin; and the MA in Communications/Television Production, University of Illinois-Chicago Campus.

Shown on the cover is *OM!* a montage painting Author Judith Hensel created for a one-person exhibition celebrating *"The Animal-Human Spiritual Connection"* held in Boulder, Colorado.

www.ingramcontent.com/pod-product-compliance
Lightning Source LLC
Chambersburg PA
CBHW050750250626
47155CB00005B/1997